CRIMINAL MINDS: JUMP CUT

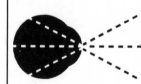

This Large Print Book carries the
Seal of Approval of N.A.V.H.

BASED ON THE CBS TELEVISION SERIES
CREATED BY JEFF DAVIS

CRIMINAL MINDS:
JUMP CUT

MAX ALLAN COLLINS

THORNDIKE PRESS

An imprint of Thomson Gale, a part of The Thomson Corporation

Detroit • New York • San Francisco • New Haven, Conn. • Waterville, Maine • London

LIBRARY OF CONGRESS CATALOGING-IN-PUBLICATION DATA

Collins, Max Allan.
   Criminal minds : jump cut / by Max Allan Collins ; based on the CBS television series created by Jeff Davis.
      p. cm.
   ISBN-13: 978-1-4104-0426-8 (hardcover : alk. paper)
   ISBN-10: 1-4104-0426-9 (hardcover : alk. paper)
   1. United States. Federal Bureau of Investigation — Fiction. 2. Criminal profilers — Fiction. 3. Criminal investigation — Fiction. 4. Large type books. I. Davis, Jeff. II. Criminal minds (Television program) III. Title.
PS3553.O4753C75 2008
813'.54—dc22   2007044615

Published in 2008 by arrangement with NAL Signet,
a member of Penguin Group (USA) Inc.

Printed in the United States of America on permanent paper
10 9 8 7 6 5 4 3 2 1

I would like to acknowledge
my assistant on this work,
co-plotter/researcher
Matthew V. Clemens.
Further acknowledgments appear
at the conclusion of this novel.

M.A.C.

*For Steve Moes —
location, location, location*

PROLOGUE:
LAWRENCE, KANSAS

Post-break, spring in a college town is energetic and fast-paced, students operating on all cylinders, finals scant weeks away, the focus on getting ready for semester's end and the summer to follow. Giddy memories of girls and boys gone wild fade away as do the doldrums of winter drudgery. As instinctive rites of spring kick in, the kids are hitting the books and the bars and on each other. All in all, a very cool time to live in a college town.

That is, unless you're not a student, or one of the year-round gainfully employed citizens of respectable Lawrence, Kansas, and are instead one of nearly two hundred homeless haunting the downtown streets and shadows of this idyllic Midwestern city of eighty-one thousand.

Human ghosts, ignored, invisible. And when they disappear, no one seems to care.

Almost no one.

■ ■ ■ ■

Glen Berten still sometimes had trouble accepting that he was homeless. To him it was not a condition, not a state of his being, rather a technicality, a temporary turn of circumstance.

As he shuffled down Winthrop Street toward Seventh, morning warmth on his face, he wore his only clothes — a blue KU hat picked up off the street last September after a drunk student dropped it, a well-worn army fatigue jacket with the name HENSON stenciled over the pocket (six bucks at a Goodwill store last November), a Chiefs T-shirt that had once been red and now so dirty it became maroon, and tattered designer jeans. His tennis shoes had been traded, along with an entire carton of cigarettes, for a pair of raggedy work boots that were only half a size too small. Wear had loosened them up fine.

Only eighteen months ago, at thirty years of age, Glen had everything — a smart, beautiful wife (Beth) and a respectable, respected career teaching high school (he held an English degree from a small, private college in Iowa), with tenure at work and a loving family life seemingly in the cards.

But the cards had a different idea.

A Texas Hold 'em player who'd started playing for fun online, Glen watched, with an odd detachment, as his hobby turned into an obsession that claimed his money, his job, his wife and even a future that had once seemed as sunny as this fine Kansas morning.

Even those first few nights, sleeping in his Camry — after Beth finally got fed up with his lying ways and gambling debts and threw him out — he'd figured it would only be a short time before he was back on his feet and winning Beth back.

He had been wrong.

Soon he got fired for pilfering money from another teacher's purse to pay off a gambling debt (the only luck Glen had run into, about then, was the school administration not calling the cops). Then, finally, the repo man had tracked him down and took away the car that had become his home, and suddenly a successful young teacher was penniless, without any shelter, with only hopelessness in good supply.

Suicide crossed his mind then, and — after several long sleepless nights of contemplation — he had climbed the fire escape of the public library looking for access to the roof to throw himself off. Once up there,

11

though, he ran into two other homeless guys who called the library roof home. Thinking he'd come up there to steal their meager belongings, the pair jumped Glen and beat hell out of him, interrupting his suicide attempt only to try to throw him off the roof themselves.

He had thought himself ready to die, but instinct kicked in and suddenly he was fighting for his life, the attack awakening a fire to live he'd thought long since extinguished. Now he slugged and kicked with a tenacity he didn't know he possessed, and managed to escape.

Over a year since that epiphany, he still found himself living on the streets; but now, if not accepting of his circumstances, he was at least better equipped to deal with them, and held out hope for an eventual return to a normal life.

A few things about the life of a homeless man had taken him by surprise. Not eating regularly, he had of course gotten skinnier, but he was stunned by how fast his muscles deteriorated. He'd been a runner once and had been in decent physical shape right up to when his life fell apart; but now he doubted he could run five blocks, let alone five miles.

As his body slipped into starvation mode,

it began using fewer calories and started burning lean tissue and holding on to the fatty stores. Consequently, he was less fit, and his six-pack abs had softened into a twelve-pack.

Now, simple survival was job one.

He had shocked himself by living through the frigid Kansas winter. Glen had eaten out of Dumpsters, panhandled, and, most nights, managed to find a bed in one of the two shelters in town. Neither had enough cots to come anywhere close to housing all the homeless, but Glen took care of himself first.

On the nights he had not made it to the shelter in time, he had gone back to the library, avoiding the roof, sleeping on the grates behind the building that provided exhaust for the boilers. Several others always jockeyed for position with him, with Glen walking the fine line between sharing bodily heat and setting yourself up for getting rolled in your sleep, or worse.

With spring here now, however, other places to sleep became available, offering more privacy, which meant more safety. Last night, for instance, he'd spent under some bushes in Buford Watson Junior Park. Most of the time, sleeping during the day was safer, but now and then he found a secure place to catch a nighttime nap.

Even though Lawrence had cracked down, thinking they could legislate the homeless out of business, Glen still managed to squeak by. Aggressive panhandling laws, plus anti-homeless ordinances — against rooftop trespassing and sleeping or sitting on sidewalks downtown — made life harder. But what the city fathers didn't seem to understand was that the homeless population had not moved to the downtown streets because they had suddenly grown tired of their luxury digs in Overland Park.

And yet, on some weird but very real level, Glen relished this life. Though his current circumstances lacked the creature comforts of his straight days, something about the streets touched the part of Glen that had led him here.

This was the ultimate gamble, wasn't it? The rush every gambler sought, though most were content to wager mere money. Every day, Glen went all in, to quote a term from the card game that had helped him destroy his old life. Dawn to dusk, dusk to dawn, he bet it all — life or death, survival or starvation, survival or freezing to death, survival or running into that one guy crazy enough and bad enough to shank Glen for his gloves, boots, or a Dumpster-scored pizza crust.

Though he would barely admit it to himself, and certainly never to another person, Glen was into this new lifestyle. In his heart, he knew he was playing for higher stakes than any of the lame-o's who had beaten him out of something as mundane as money.

As an English major, he told himself he was researching the novel that he would one day write to climb into a better life than he'd ever had.

Too early for this shit, but here we are anyway. Pickings are thin this morning. There's that loser across the street in the army jacket. Why does he have the damned cap pulled down so low? We can't even see his face. Be nice to snap a photo of him, but that damned cap. . . .

Where the hell is he going?

Dude's definitely a bum. Hasn't seen a bath since God knows when. Isn't all that big — we can probably take him down without much trouble. Last thing we need is more trouble. . . . That *last* one, Jesus. . . .

This one will be easier though. We'll be better this time than the last. We've practiced this time. We practiced our lines and, anyway, we're experienced now. . . .

This guy, we got him cold. That is, if he's the right one for us, of course. Still some

15

scouting to do. He's not that good-looking, but he's got a little something about him says he's not mister average down-and-outer.

We're careful not to let the army jacket dude see us. We stay in the shadows on the other side of the street as he moseys down Winthrop. We like his build, but it's hard to see much from this distance. Plus, the beard. *That* has to go.

Now what? Army jacket dude is turning down the alley that runs from Winthrop over to Sixth. Why the hell is he doing *that?* Sixth's a hell of a lot busier. If we want this guy, we don't want to approach him right in the middle of morning rush hour. There are some people and some cars on Seventh, sure, but nothing like on Sixth. We think about letting him go. Then again. . . .

The alley provides us, maybe, with an opportunity. . . .

Still, why is he going there? We picked him up coming out of the park. If he had wanted to go to Sixth, why the hell not go the opposite direction from the park? He would've been there in a block's walk.

No, got to be another reason.

What could be down that alley? We look both ways and cross the street as the army jacket dude moves deeper into the alley. Less light in there, harder to see him.

But that's going to make us harder to see, too, right?

Edge up to the corner of a brick building, peek around into the alley. Army jacket dude is about halfway down on the left side. What *building* is that he's behind?

Oh yeah, Sal's, the pizzeria! Army jacket dude's going Dumpster diving.

Is this the time we should take him?

We're about to make a decision when a squad car turns into the alley — cops must have seen army jacket, too. They're going down there to give him shit. We don't need to watch what happens, we've made our decision.

We'll keep hunting.

Nobody in Lawrence seemed to know her name.

Most everyone called her "Bag Lady," even though she had a grocery cart. In her forties, most of the cops figured, but she was so unkempt, it was hard to tell. Slightly over five feet, Bag Lady's build was slim and her gray-streaked long brown hair was mostly stuffed under a frayed knit stocking cap. She wore ratty jeans, hole-stippled tennis shoes, a series of three or four shirts, and (in winter) an overcoat so long it dragged on the ground. The grocery cart, filled with all manner of treasure-trash scrounged over the last two years (including six Bibles), was her only companion.

The police had picked up Bag Lady a few times, but they soon discovered she had both bipolar disorder and schizophrenia. She'd been hospitalized twice, but she would refuse her meds and before long she'd be back on the streets and just as far around the bend as before she went in.

She wandered a fairly large landscape, but the borders might as well have been twenty-foot concrete walls, for she would not venture one step beyond them. Her domain was defined by the railroad tracks along Constant Park on the north, the Amtrak station on the east, Ninth Street on the south and Louisiana Street on the west.

When her bipolar lows set in, Bag Lady might hunker down for days at a time, somehow sustaining herself on whatever she kept inside that grocery cart. The bipolar highs, on the other hand, saw Bag Lady in the streets, talking to herself, marching up and down the pavement, raving to whoever would listen about the coming of the Antichrist ("He'll be Jewish, has to be Jewish!") and how the reestablishment of Israel in 1948 set in motion the "beginning of the end times."

She would use a rudimentary sign language to share her message with passing motorists. First, Bag Lady would spread her hands to represent the world, then she would rub one index finger over the other in a "shame on you" gesture to represent the Antichrist, then she would steeple her fingers to show that prayer was the only way . . . and, if the motorist still didn't get the message, she would point to the sky. Heaven was the answer. Such behavior was reserved for street people and the heads of churches.

Several of the patrol officers knew the pantomime and had heard her spiel often enough to know that Bag Lady never deviated from her message, and while she might be nuttier than a Baby Ruth bar, she was basically harmless, though there had been more than one fender bender involving motorists startled by the gesticulating lady with the grocery cart.

She knew that at one time she'd had a name; she just didn't remember it now. The cops all called her Bag Lady and that seemed good enough for her. She had long ago stopped worrying about whatever her parents used to call her, forty-some years ago. The Lord was her pilot now.

Though she could not recall its author,

she remembered reading a book called *God Is My Co-Pilot,* a long, long time ago. She figured that if God was flying with her, wouldn't it be smarter to have an all-knowing, all-seeing deity in charge all the time, instead of just when something catastrophic happened to the regular pilot? Co-pilot wasn't enough. Pass the goggles to God!

That plan had worked pretty well so far. The Almighty had chosen her to pass along His message (her message, too, now). She would be rewarded like the prophet she was, after a lifetime wandering the wilderness and spreading the Word. God would give her a brand-new, glorious name when she finally passed through the gates into His kingdom. For now, until The End came (any day now), she would simply be the vessel through which the message passed.

She saw how people looked at her, like she was sick or frightening, but she chalked that up to them either not getting her message, or getting it completely and realizing they were on the wrong side of God's good graces. No wonder they were terrified! She would be, too, if she hadn't made peace and let God guide her life years ago.

Today, she wanted to get her message out near the library. The first thing she needed to do was find some breakfast. Normally, nothing would stand between her and the day's work. After all, He would provide. The problem was, He had not got around to providing for a few days now, and she felt herself growing weaker.

Yesterday, a passerby had slipped her a dollar, but that did her no good. She couldn't eat money and the only thing a buck would get her was a candy bar. God would want her to eat better than a Crunch bar, wouldn't He?

She strolled along Sixth, pushing her cart in front of her, aware of the stares of the passersby, but doing her best to ignore them, Onward Christian soldiering toward the alley. Her long overcoat lay folded up in the cart, the warmth of the spring morning a welcome change from what had been a hard winter, even for Lawrence.

"I am Alpha and Omega, the beginning and the end, the first and last," she said as she walked, barely aware the words were coming out of her mouth, the Message second nature now.

The verses kept coming as she moved through the light pedestrian traffic.

"For without are dogs and sorcerers and whoremongers and murderers and idolaters and whosoever loveth and maketh a lie."

As she passed, they all parted to let her through.

"I, Jesus, have sent mine angel to testify unto you these things in the churches. I am the root. . . ."

Just as she was about to turn down the alley, a patrol car emerged from the shadows, almost clipping her cart as it nosed out into the street. In the backseat, she glimpsed a young man she had seen around before. She didn't know him by name, but recognized his army coat and KU cap. She continued her recitation as the car passed and the man in the backseat gave her a wan smile.

Turning down the alley toward Sal's Pizzeria — and what was usually a treasure trove of a Dumpster — she said, "He which testifieth these things saith, 'Surely I come quickly.' Amen. Even so, come Jesus. The grace of our Lord Jesus Christ be with you all. Amen."

He would not provide bread and wine for her, but she was pretty sure He would point her to some pizza crust.

That was a close call with the cops!

Just as well — that guy looked like he'd be a pain in the ass to deal with, anyway. We're better off.

What's *this* now? *She* might do. Kind of old,

and we'll probably have to pry that fucking cart away from her . . . but she might work.

We'll just duck into this doorway until she gets closer. She can't see us, can she? . . . Oh, shit, she's looking right at us . . . and . . . she's still coming, but you can tell now she's got no idea we're here! We watch as she moves toward the Dumpster in the middle of the alley.

Who the hell is she *talking* to?

We glance around, but see no one else in the alley but her and us. Oh! She's talking to *herself.*

She says, "For without are dogs and sorcerers and whoremongers and murderers and idolaters and whosoever loveth and maketh a lie."

Great! A loon. Still . . . maybe. . . .

She climbs into the Dumpster and disappears. She's in there for a while, rooting around probably, only we start to wonder if maybe she's decided to take a nap or something. We're just about to move out of our doorway and get a closer look when her head pops out, and her mouth and chin are covered with tomato sauce. She's found a pizza in the trash and seems to have rubbed the damned thing all over herself!

Nuts *and* a mess. We need a woman, we could really use a woman . . . but not *this* one.

We'll keep looking.

Bengie Gray was terrified.

He had flunked out of KU at the semester and the pudgy freshman hadn't had the nerve to go home. His parents — family farmers in Nebraska — had scrimped most of their lives to send their son to college and he had promptly laid an egg bigger than any of the hens at home ever managed.

Away from home for the first time, lonely, homesick, and ostracized by the college community because . . . well . . . he didn't know why. He knew he wasn't cool, that much was sure — never had been; but something about him had rubbed his room-mates in the dorm the wrong way, and the word had spread from there.

It seemed no matter how hard he tried to make friends, he couldn't. Not for the most part anyway. A couple of guys — freshmen geekier even than he was, if that was possible — who worked with him in the dining hall as part of the work-study program? They accepted him. That was about it.

When the university had asked Bengie to vacate the dorm, leave his work-study job, and disappear from their campus, the pair of fellow geeks had given him a home until just after the new year started. But even they had turned their backs on Bengie — *"Dude, get a job!"* — and he had been left to the streets.

The winter had been hard, but Bengie wasn't a complete moron. He *had* gotten a job — working evenings in a sandwich shop. Problem was, he didn't make enough money to make a down payment on an apartment, so he couldn't find a place to live. He went to the shelters when he could, mingled with the bums and their urine smell, and slept in the Laundromat while he washed his work clothes; he would wash his hair in the sink in the bathroom of the sandwich shop, and generally was doing okay except for not having enough money to find a home.

That, and his utter shame at flunking out.

He still called his parents on Sunday nights, usually on the Laundromat pay phone (collect of course), and lied to them about school and tests and girlfriends.

They had told him how much they were looking forward to seeing him at spring break. That week he had phoned them to tell them his new girlfriend had invited him to go home with her. They were disappointed, sure, but his parents understood, and were probably relieved he *had* a girl, and told him they couldn't wait for him coming home for the summer.

On this fine spring morning, walking in the same direction as the one-way traffic on Kentucky, Bengie still hadn't come up with a lie to explain to his folks why he would not be home for the summer.

Or maybe he *could* go home. Maybe he could pretend he was looking forward to his sophomore year, and would find a "summer" job back home and then simply tell his parents he'd decided he liked working at . . . at whatever it was . . . and about there the fantasy broke down.

But getting a better job was no fantasy. Today, his goal was to get online at the public library and post his résumé, and get something that would make him enough money to actually live on. Spring seemed to have gotten him jazzed a little bit, and he was actually feeling like he was turning a corner, both literally and figuratively, as he rounded the corner onto Seventh, the library only a block away now.

This was it, he told himself.

Today, his life would change forever.

Maybe this isn't our day.

First, the army jacket dude damn near leads us straight into the arms of the cops, then that broad with the cart turns out to be crazier than a shit-house mouse.

26

We *really* wanted to land somebody today.

A schedule is, after all, a schedule. We can always wait, tomorrow's another day and all that — we might get lucky with a fresh start. . . .

We come out of the shadows and the crazy lady sees us. She ducks down into the Dumpster like a prairie dog in its hole. No way we're dealing with a nutcase like that. Assuming we could bag her, there's no guarantee she could perform without taking enough roofies to knock down a horse.

So, screw her and the Dumpster she dove in on.

We'll do without for today. We want to keep to schedule, but not at the risk of ruining the whole project. Being self-funded, going independent, gives us a certain leeway, a freedom others could only envy.

Moving back down the alley toward Seventh, we catch a glimpse of a kid walking past the alley. He's on the chunky side, but just might fit the bill. He's trying to not seem homeless, but they have a *look* about them, don't they?

We move to the edge of the alley and peek around. He's heading in the direction of the library. It would be better if we had time to thin him up a little — would probably help; but you have to settle, sometimes, when you're trying to make a schedule.

Falling in behind, we follow him for the half block to the library and watch him turn up the concrete stairs toward the front door.

He'll do, but if he gets inside, we'll either have to grab him in there, or wait for him to come out.

Seeing the security camera mounted on the corner of the roof, we decide the only two choices are to call it a day or find an inconspicuous place to wait and watch for him to come back out. The coffee shop on the corner across the street makes our decision for us.

After two double espressos, the door of the library opens and our man steps out. He's even younger than we thought! That's good, that's lucky. We snap a couple of quick photos with the camera phone and go outside. He's heading back in the direction he came from earlier.

We follow at a distance for a block or two. He stops outside a restaurant looking longingly through the window. He's hungry.

That's good too.

Walking up to him, we pull the wad of bills from our pocket and let him see it. His eyes are the size of the jumbo pies over at Sal's.

"Hey, buddy — want to make some fast cash?

"Look, I . . . I'm straight. No offense."

"None taken — anyway, it's not like that, man."

"I don't want anything to do with drugs. I don't use them and I won't sell them."

"Look, bro! This is a job offer. It's legal, it's easy . . . and you can make a hundred bucks for five hours' work."

"I . . . I don't know about this. You better —"

"Let's go inside, have some breakfast, and talk about it. You don't want the money then, that's fine. Either way, you get a square meal out of the deal."

He can't take his eyes off the money.

We have him. It's that easy.

"Oh . . . okay," he says. "I'll talk to you, let you buy me breakfast. But no promises."

"None expected — oh, shit! Gotta feed the meter before *we* get fed — walk and talk, okay? Car's just around the corner. Fill you in about the job."

Eyes still on the money, he nods.

He's ours.

"In films murders are always very clean,"
Alfred Hitchcock said.
"But what a messy thing it is
to kill a man."

CHAPTER ONE

Situated on the United States Marine Corps Base at Quantico, Virginia, the FBI Academy — known by those who work, teach and train there as the Facility — sprawls over 385 woodland acres that provide the privacy and security required for the FBI's operational functions and training.

At the Facility, the Behavioral Analysis Unit operates as part of the FBI's Training and Development Division, consulting with law enforcement across the nation on crimes requiring the skills of the BAU's top profilers.

Supervisory Special Agent Aaron Hotchner — broad-shouldered but slender, with black hair, brown eyes and the kind of chiseled features whose somber concern could be misread as unkind — hunkered over his desk. His suit coat, which almost never came off at work, was hung with precision over the back of his chair.

As masculine as its occupant, the spacious office informed any visitor that this was a serious man not just successful at anything he attempted, but excelling at it. Witness three sets of mahogany shelves lining the wall behind his desk, home to numerous trophies for various skilled activities, including several for marksmanship. Note the wall opposite, arrayed with framed diplomas, citations, and the seal of the Federal Bureau of Investigation.

Not to be trifled with, Agent Hotchner.

Sharing the wall with the door was a picture window whose venetian blinds were kept slanted open so that Hotchner could monitor the sunken bullpen of the Behavioral Analysis Unit beyond. The wall opposite the door held three long, narrow columns of bulletproof glass charitably referred to as windows, although (short of an acetylene torch) they had no way to open, their sole function letting in light, which they performed well for the north side of the building with its limited sunshine.

His normally grave mein approaching morose, Hotchner — not quite forty — was in a dark place, the kind that in throwing light upon only reveals further darkness: specifically, he was poring over statistics from thirty-seven school shootings in the United States and Canada over the last ten years.

No such thing, he well knew, as an accurate school shooter profile.

There was, of course, the media-driven image of the trench-coated loners à la Harris and Klebold in Columbine; but Hotchner knew the image was just that, a myth created by the perpetrators themselves and perpetuated by a media responsible only to ratings, not society.

He was hoping to develop a more accurate profile in order to prevent future attacks. The task seemed impossible, but Hotchner had never backed down from a challenge, starting with the third-grade bully a certain kindergartner had stood up to in a school yard. Truth was, backing down, giving up, just wasn't in his DNA.

He had lost battles; all warriors did — but he had never surrendered.

One of the preliminary stats surprised him. Nineteen of the thirty-seven cases, over half, occurred in the spring, including the latest, just a few weeks ago when thirty-two college students and their killer perished at Virginia Tech.

For those who felt a school shooter had to be an ostracized loner, the springtime shootings would just give them more . . . the word sprang to mind unbidden . . . ammunition. Spring shootings implied that students who had been bullied and ostracized, if only in their own minds, had taken the abuse for as long as they could, then snapped.

As a seasoned FBI profiler, Hotchner knew some stressor would invariably emerge in any of these cases that could be labeled the proverbial "last straw"; but very few people really just "snapped."

Most of these actions were painstakingly planned. They took time, effort, focus and perseverance. In those shootings, the killers didn't just "snap" — premeditated murder, particularly on such a scale, did not imply someone out of control, rather *in* control, and seeking complete control over life and mostly death, turning twisted delusion into tragic reality.

Hotchner was studying further stats when a knock at his door interrupted.

Frankly relieved for a moment away from his grim work, he looked up. "Come in."

Special Agent Jennifer "JJ" Jareau entered. In her mid-twenties, Jareau looked especially young today, her blonde hair back in a loose ponytail, her blue eyes bright, her skin pale and fresh — she might have been a college student herself.

But she was not — rather she was the BAU's local law enforcement liaison, as professional as her crisp black suit and white blouse. Her sober expression mirrored Hotchner's as she approached his desk, a file folder in her left hand.

Hotchner knew from experience that when this pleasant young woman took on a grave demeanor, nothing good was on its way.

"Yes?"

"We just got a call from Detective Rob Learman," she said, "with the Lawrence, Kansas PD — has a case he's requested our help on."

"Let's hear it."

Without sitting, referring not at all to the file folder, she laid out the details in quick, no-nonsense fashion. Her other duties included handling media and she could reduce a complex case to headline-news highlights.

Hotchner drew air in through his nose, let it out the same way. "I'll take the file. Call Detective Learman and say yes. Then gather the whole team — conference in one hour."

"No problem," she said. "I'll be prepared to present the facts."

Hotchner almost smiled. "I know."

Alone, the profiler read the copy of the

Lawrence PD's case file cover to cover. Then he read it again. He did not have the near-photographic memory of his young colleague, Dr. Reid, and often took a second pass with important documents.

But by the time he got to the conference room, Hotchner had the file down cold, his mind already cataloguing details about the UnSub — FBI-speak for the unknown subject behind these crimes.

He'd spent extra time on the crime scene photos and the autopsy protocol, including the preliminary tox screen and stomach contents that showed signs of Rohypnol. Local police reports were frequently lacking in victimology and demographics of the area around the crime scene. Either the locals were writing reports for people who already knew these things or, more often, simply did not understand how important such elements were to solving these types of crimes.

The conference room with its dark maroon walls was dominated by a round mahogany conference table with six high-back chairs. As in Hotchner's office, a picture window with venetian blinds looked out upon the expansive bullpen. A wall-mounted whiteboard just inside the door still contained scribbles from a previous case, but the wall with the flat-screen TV (next to a bulletin board of maps, circulars, photos and so on) had the attention of the seated agents of the BAU team.

Their newest member, Special Agent Emily Prentiss, sat nearest the door. The lanky thirty-something Prentiss carried the kind of sharp-featured attractiveness often wedded to keen intelligence, her reddish-tinged dark brown hair cut as straight as that of an ancient Egyptian princess. Like Jareau, she wore a dark suit.

Still somewhat of an outsider, Prentiss had joined the unit under less than ideal circumstances — unlike the rest of his team, she had not been handpicked by Hotchner; rather she had been foisted upon him when a former, valued member unexpectedly flamed out. Yale-educated and the daughter of an ambassador — and with vague high-level political connections that frankly unsettled Hotchner — Prentiss had spent ten years working in the St. Louis and Chicago field offices before her new assignment.

To her left sat Jareau, next to whom perched Dr. Spencer Reid, conspicuously the youngest member of the team. Only twenty-five and yet already in his fourth year with the FBI, Reid held doctoral degrees in Chemistry, Mathematics, and Engineering.

Brown-eyed with longish brown hair that cut his forehead in a thick comma, Reid had pleasant, boyish features hardened by his horn-rimmed glasses, and was prone to birdlike gestures that reflected energy, not nerves.

An only child with an IQ of 187 and capable of reading in the neighborhood of twenty thousand words per minute, the young man had the fashion sense and social skills of a middle-school student. Today's ensemble was a gray plaid short-sleeve dress shirt with a red-and-yellow striped tie, loosened slightly, collar of the shirt unbuttoned; his chinos were a little big on him.

Dead serious about his job — and for that matter everything in his life (including assorted Certified Nerd/Geek interests) — Reid managed to maintain a puppy-dog enthusiasm despite the horrible things he'd witnessed on the job.

Separated from Prentiss by an empty chair sat Supervisory Special Agent Derek Morgan, in a dark blue shirt unbuttoned a ways, and even darker blue slacks. Thirty-three and biracial (mother white, father African-American), the ex-Chicago cop had a law degree from Northwestern University (thanks to a full-ride football scholarship) and had been with the Bureau for seven years, coming over from ATF. His athletic build — consistent with his black belt in martial arts and his occasional role as a teacher of self-defense classes here at Quantico — stopped short of muscle-bound, and in fact he displayed an almost balletic grace.

Wickedly handsome with a killer smile, Morgan made friends wherever he went, with never a shortage of interest from the opposite sex; but the sparkling eyes and flashing teeth were a wall few got behind. Morgan's personal life took a backseat to his devotion to his job, the agent as driven in his way as Hotchner, and this was perhaps why the latter trusted the former so implicitly.

Hotchner himself was the last to sit.

Directly across from him was the senior member of their team, Supervisory Special Agent Jason Gideon, looking almost casual as he sat back in a wine-colored long-sleeved shirt and dark blue trousers, right ankle resting on his left knee. His short-sheared black hair, his hawklike nose and firm jaw, and thoughtful compassionate eyes under thick black slashes of eyebrow, added up to something strong but not harsh, an oblong face grooved by smiles and laughter that had not taken place on the job.

An FBI agent since 1978, the fiftyish Gideon — whose quiet, professorly demeanor seemed at odds with a broad-shouldered build — was a living legend in the BAU, one of a handful of pioneering profilers whose work had spawned a whole new way of detection.

By all rights Gideon, not Hotchner, should be heading up the team; and Hotchner was well aware that his leadership, if not his position, had more or less been deferred to him by the older, more experienced agent. A six-month medical leave for post-traumatic stress disorder had kept Gideon out of the field, and off the roster as team leader. When he returned, the senior agent made no effort to take Hotchner's position, and no rivalry existed between the two.

Still, Gideon's status gave him a special leeway and he would issue orders almost as frequently as Hotchner himself. The two had established respect for each other long ago, and Hotchner considered Gideon's wisdom and experience key tools in their crime-solving arsenal.

Here, seated around a table that might have been in a conference room at a bank or an insurance agency, were the top behavioral analysts in America, the profilers whose speciality was to go wherever and whenever local law enforcement found itself up against a criminal mind requiring expert investigation.

Without preamble or niceties, Hotchner said, "JJ got a call from the Lawrence, Kansas, PD. They think they're dealing with a serial killer."

"They think?" Morgan asked, brow furrowed. "Don't they know?"

"Someone's stalking homeless people."

Reid sat forward and squinted in thought. "The predator's perfect victim — preying on the weakest members of the herd."

"It may not be as simple as that," Hotchner said. He turned to the liaison officer. "JJ?"

Jareau took control of the meeting, punching the remote for the wall-mounted monitor, a still image jumping on: a crime scene photo of a man on his stomach on wooden flooring.

Her dark eyes unblinking and wide, Prentiss said, "I thought you said the victims were *homeless* people."

This victim clearly wore a business suit. Dark stains, obviously blood, splotched most of his back.

Hotchner gave Prentiss a small, sharp look that said, *Let JJ explain.*

"This *is* a homeless man," Jareau said. "Roger Rondell, arrested in Lawrence once for vagrancy and twice for panhandling — no felonies on his record. Just found this morning, in a condemned abandoned house."

Eyebrows up, Morgan said, "Pretty nice threads for a homeless dude."

The crime scene photo gave way to another.

The victim had been turned on his back now, the picture concentrating on his face: clean-shaven, hair clipped and not noticeably dirty. Easier to tell in this photo that the collar of the suit was slightly stained and not by blood; but the clothing still looked suspiciously nice.

"Pretty clean, too," Morgan added. "Figure he'd only have one suit like that, maybe another, and keeping them clean wouldn't be easy, on the streets."

"That's what separates this from any homeless killings on record," Hotchner said, looking from the screen to his agents and back again. "In Lawrence, homeless people are disappearing, then turning up stabbed and slashed . . . but also spruced up."

"Spruced up?" Prentiss parroted skeptically.

"Cleaned up. Bathed or showered or whatever. And wearing new clothes. Or possibly secondhand clothes, but fairly nice ones, freshly laundered."

Fingers fluttering on his cheek, Reid said, "You said, 'homeless people' — does that mean the killer's victims are of both sexes?"

They all knew that the odds of any sexual component to the crimes went down if the victims weren't exclusively male or female.

"This is an equal-opportunity killer," Jareau said, working the remote.

Three more close-ups of dead faces popped up on the screen.

With Rondell, the quartet now consisted of two men and two women. Both men and one of the women were white, but the other woman was African-American. Their ages seemed varied, too, judging by their faces.

"Homelessness," Hotchner said, "is the only common factor."

Thinking out loud in his halting, considered fashion, a frowning Reid dug a fist under his chin and said, "Most serial killers are *white* . . . but even when they're not, almost all choose victims within their own race."

Morgan's eyes were wide; he flipped a hand, an almost dismissive gesture. "This guy's all over the map! Men, women, young, and *not* so young, black, white . . ."

"I trust you use 'guy,' " Reid said, "as a

non-sexually specific designation."

Morgan gave Reid the "are you kidding me?" look, but all the agents knew what Reid meant: while female serial killers were rare, they were hardly unknown.

Hotchner pointed at the display of victims and said, "We might have an obsessive factor here — an alternating killer."

"How so?" Morgan asked.

Hotchner moved his head a fraction — a shrug for him. "Every other victim has been a woman — specifically, numbers one and three. Number two was the other man, Rondell our fourth."

"What about timing," Prentiss said, studying the screen like hieroglyphics she was trying to make out. "How far apart are the crimes?"

Jareau said, "First was late October, one in November, then none until two weeks ago — finally today, the Rondell murder."

"Time frame's all over the map, too," Morgan said, shaking his head.

"Any sign of sexual sadism?" Reid asked.

Despite the unlikelihood of a sexual element, this needed to be asked.

Hotchner shook his head. "The Lawrence crime scene analysts did get DNA off the first victim, but that was it. Otherwise, evidence has been hard to come by. One significant find, however: all four victims tested positive for Rohypnol."

Reid squinted, as if the flat-screen had gone fuzzy. "Roofies," he said, almost to himself, as if tasting the word. "Date-rape drug. Yet no sexual component?"

Hotchner nodded. "The perp might drug his victims to subdue them initially, but there's that other strange factor: the cleaning up, the haircuts, shaving them. . . . This killer most likely used the drug to make the victims compliant, pliable."

"Makes sense," Prentiss said, nodding.

"I still don't get why he's tidying them up," Morgan said.

Gideon had been sitting back in his chair, gazing over his tented fingertips. Now he sat up straight and spoke in a soft but commanding voice, and his hands began to rub together, as if working up heat.

"Maybe," Gideon said, "he thinks he's saving them."

With a lilt in his voice, as if suggesting they all order wings at TGIF, Reid said, "Baptizing the unwashed before sending them to meet their Maker?"

"Something like that. Something ritualistic, possibly."

Prentiss sat forward, head cocked as she asked, "Does that mean our murderer thinks homelessness is some kind of sin?"

Gideon shrugged and lifted an open hand. "We dealt with that 'house cleaner' killer in Kansas City. This might be a similar pathology, yes."

Eyes tight, Prentiss asked, "Will this UnSub devolve into that same sort of killing machine?"

"I don't know," Gideon admitted. "We're just thinking out loud, so far." His eyes went to Jareau. "Have we identified all the victims?"

Jareau said, "Not yet. The most recent victim, found in that abandoned house, is Rondell. The first, a female, was . . ." She checked her notes. ". . . Elizabeth Hawkins. Thirty-two with several arrests for prostitution, panhandling, and vagrancy. She was found two days before Halloween."

"Kansas doesn't seem like a very friendly environment to homeless people," Morgan said.

Reid responded to the dark joke with facts: "Lawrence, Kansas, is second on an Internet list of cities that are the 'meanest' to homeless people in the United States. Only Sarasota, Florida, is regarded more unfriendly to the homeless."

Morgan had a stunned expression, not expecting his wisecrack to be verifiable.

"You just carry this stuff around in your head?"

The slender Reid shrugged. "Where else would you suggest?"

"Don't tempt me. . . ."

Gideon cut in: "What about the other two victims?"

Jareau checked her notes again. "The other woman, Paula Creston, African-American, late twenties — arrested once for shoplifting a loaf of bread and some cold cuts from a convenience store." She looked up at her colleagues. "Creston was found two weeks ago. The other male vic, the one found in November, is a John Doe. The medical examiner puts his age at fifty-two or so, and there was no fingerprint match on AFIS, nor in VICAP."

"Have we tried the military?" Hotchner asked.

Jareau said, "Garcia's on it, even as we speak."

This got a brief smile from everyone, except Gideon, who remained focused on the crimes.

The Garcia in question was Audio/Visual Technician Penelope Garcia, their digital intelligence analyst and all-around computer whiz. A computer prodigy in her early thirties, cute, pleasantly plump, stylishly punky, Garcia seldom left her self-proclaimed "Office of Unfettered Omniscience" (but when she did, it was usually behind the wheel of her vintage Cadillac convertible).

"Military is a good start," Gideon said.

"But you know the DOD," Jareau said, glumly. "They're in no hurry to cooperate."

Hotchner said, "I've got a friend over at the Department of Defense — maybe I can grease the wheels for her."

"You've got *friends,* Hotch," Morgan said with a little grin. "Good to hear."

Hotchner flicked a smile at Morgan, a major concession.

Gideon asked, "How close to Thanksgiving was the November crime?"

"Two weeks before," Jareau answered.

That precocious kid in the back row who drove everybody crazy in school, Reid popped in again. "What about victimology?"

Jareau said, "You already have it, as far as it goes — only things the victims had in common is that they were homeless, and kept mostly to downtown Lawrence."

"They disappeared from an area where they should have been relatively safe," Hotchner said. "The downtown area was their home. Lawrence is fairly typical in this regard — the downtown of a city is the domain of the homeless: public buildings to get out of the weather, restaurants that provide a source of food."

"They also *feel* safe in their domain," Gideon pointed out.

"But the nature of their existence is by definition an unsafe one," Hotchner countered. "They would be naturally suspicious of anyone who doesn't look like he or she belongs."

"However," Gideon said, head tilted slightly, "the downtown provides our UnSub with two vital enablers."

"What's that?" Jareau asked.

"Availability and vulnerability," Gideon said, with a one-two of his fingers. His eyes tightened under the dark slashes of brow. "Where were the bodies found?"

"The first, Elizabeth Hawkins," Jareau said, "was discovered in an abandoned factory. Body found by workers coming in to remove asbestos. Number two, John Doe, was in a Dumpster behind a grocery store, discovered by a bag boy taking out some trash. Paula Creston, victim number three, turned up in a junkyard. The last, Rondell, of course, was found in an abandoned house."

"There's got to be more," Prentiss said.

"There will be," Hotchner said, "when we

get there. In the meantime, everybody get packed up."

They all knew what this meant: the BAU's private Learjet would be waiting for them at Andrews Air Force Base.

Hotchner was saying, "They just found the latest body this morning, so we can probably get to the crime scene before dark if we hustle." He checked his wristwatch. "We're wheels up in an hour."

Late afternoon, the warm day cooling into evening, Detective Rob Learman — no one called him Robert except his mother, back when he was ten, and he hated "Bob" and "Bobby" — stood outside the unmarked police car in front of the Lawrence Municipal Airport and blew dragon streams of smoke through his nostrils. Policy no longer allowed him to smoke *in* the car, but no one had said he couldn't smoke *next* to the car.

Fortyish, with sandy hair, blue eyes, five o'clock shadow, and an all-day sardonic attitude, Learman was a good cop, and knew it. But he was Old School — follow the evidence, find the bad guy, bust his damn ass. He didn't have a lot of faith in profiling. Psychological horse hockey was his opinion of profiling, topped off with a dollop of New Age nonsense.

Puffing away in the parking lot, Learman recalled a joke a buddy had told him about profilers — specifically, about a trainee attending a profiling course.

"Logic is a very important factor in profiling," the instructor says.

"Logic?" the trainee asks.

"Yes. Let me ask you some questions. Do you own a weed whacker?"

"Yes," the trainee says.

"Well, then," the instructor says, "logic tells me that you then must have a lawn."

"Yes."

"If you have a lawn, you must have a house."

The trainee nods.

"If you have a house, odds are you're married."

"Yes!"

The instructor says, "If you have a wife, a house, and a lawn, the odds are you have kids."

The trainee nods, feeling he truly understands the lesson.

When the trainee returns to his department, one of his cohorts asks him what he has learned.

"Logic," the trainee says proudly.

"Logic?" the friend asks.

"Yeah. Let me show you. Do you own a

weed whacker?"

"No," the friend says.

"You're a homosexual."

Learman grinned at the punch line as he inhaled deeply from the cigarette. Truthfully, it wasn't far from how he felt about profiling, but the thing was, his Old School ways had gotten them exactly nowhere, and the bodies were piling up.

With four dead and the end nowhere in sight, he was ready to take help where he could get it. The FBI BAU team had caught a lot of bad guys utilizing their profiling methods, plus had a reputation for pitching in with everything from legwork to taking down perps. Maybe they were all in the same church and just sitting in different pews.

Worth a shot, anyway.

Stubbing out his cigarette, Learman saw three black Chevy Tahoes pull up to the white zone near the front doors of the small airport, and park. Three feds climbed out in their standard-issue dark suits and darker sunglasses — Kansas City field office.

Learman recognized one of them.

Square-jawed, light-blue-eyed Jeff Minet had the build of a tight end and the mind of a rocket scientist. He'd graduated from Auburn in three years, got his master's in criminology, was a cop down south for a few years, then joined the Bureau.

When Learman walked across the lot to meet the agents, Minet met the detective halfway, hand extended. They shook.

"Detective Larr-muhn," Minet said, mispronouncing Learman's name with his deep Alabama accent. "Pleasure to see you again, son."

Minet played the good ol' boy card often and well. People figured because the FBI man spoke slow, he thought slow. More than one bad guy had gone to prison with that mistake his last before a cell door clanged shut behind him.

Minet introduced Learman to the other agents, then said, "You gonna meet up with that BAU team, right?"

Learman nodded.

"Well, two of these Tahoes are for them. You wanna make sure they get 'em?"

"Isn't that your job?" Learman asked.

"Got to head back to KC, son," Minet said, flipping his set of keys to one of the other two.

Somebody handed Minet a clipboard and Learman signed for the vehicles.

"You or that BAU team need anything now, you have them give us a call, hear?"

The other two agents climbed into the

remaining Tahoe, but Learman caught Minet's sleeve. "Hold up, Jeff. You know any of these people?"

Minet nodded, and this time when he spoke, the accent all but disappeared. "Dealt with Jason Gideon once. Might be the smartest man I ever met."

Coming from somebody as smart as Minet, this was high praise. Maybe Learman had called the right people for help.

Minet continued: "Soft-spoken, this Gideon . . . but I saw him drop a two-hundred-and-fifty pounder on PCP with a short right hand."

"Good to know," Learman said. "Thanks."

"This guy Hotchner, I ran into him, too. You'll think he's a cold fish, but still waters run deep . . . and hot. He'll be the second smartest guy in town, after Gideon."

"What about me?" Learman said with a grin. "Don't I rate?"

"With this bunch around? You won't be in the top ten, buddy." Then Minet seemed to reboot the Alabama accent, saying, "Y'all be careful, and you know where to find us if needs must."

And the Kansas City FBI contingent was gone.

Learman figured he had time for one more smoke. Private planes, like the one the

BAU team used, landed on the other side of the field from the terminal, but Learman knew they would be ferried over.

He had just ground out his one-more-smoke on the sidewalk when, on cue, the double doors opened and six people walked out, each pulling a small suitcase on wheels, and lugging a shoulder bag. Traveling light, for superheroes.

And the BAU team had, lately at least — after a string of spectacular successes — indeed been painted by many in the cop trade (not to mention the national media) as virtual superheroes. And superheroes didn't need luggage.

Still, seeing them hauling their bags gave them a nicely human dimension, and suddenly Learman felt a little more like he was dealing with real people.

Two men led the sextet as they moved toward the Tahoes. The one on Learman's right was FBI from the top of his perfectly combed dark hair to the soles of his spit-shined Florsheims. He walked with confidence, erect, shoulders back despite the weight of the shoulder bag, and with an air of humorless command.

The other man in the lead looked more like a college professor than a Fed — loafers, no socks, blue jeans, an open-collar red cotton shirt and a tweed sports jacket. *What, no leather elbow patches?* This guy's face was serious but there was something in his eyes that immediately made Learman feel at ease.

Behind them were two women, one a tall, classy, quietly curvy brunette with clothes that looked more expensive than those of her shapely blonde colleague, who was slightly shorter but seemed, to Learman at least, in a better mood.

Behind them, bringing up the rear, were an athletic black man who could have been a running back for the Chiefs, and a tall, gangly kid who wore his bag over his left shoulder so that it hung under his right arm. The young man wore a sweater, a plaid shirt with a striped tie like a college kid on job shadow day.

Learman met them. "Detective Rob Learman, Lawrence PD."

The black-haired Fed extended his hand. "Supervisory Special Agent Aaron Hotchner."

They shook, the Fed's grip firm but not bone crushing; a guy this confident had nothing to prove.

"The Tahoes are unlocked," Learman said. "Three agents from the Kansas City field office left them. I signed off."

Hotchner said, "Thanks. They didn't hang around?"

"No. But Agent Minet said just call if you need anything."

"We should be fine. We're here to help, not get in your way."

"Sure. Thanks." *Right,* Learman thought, *how could five FBI agents ever get underfoot in a local investigation?*

Then he reminded himself: *You invited them here. You're the one hip-deep in homeless stiffs. . . .*

They loaded their stuff into the two remaining Tahoes. The job took about a minute and Learman got the impression they'd been through this particular activity numerous times.

Then Hotchner introduced Supervisory Special Agent Dr. Spencer Reid, Supervisory Special Agent Emily Prentiss, Supervisory Special Agent Derek Morgan and Supervisory Special Agent Jennifer Jareau, who said, "Call me JJ. I'm not a profiler — I'm the liaison between you, the FBI in general, and the BAU team in particular . . . and the media."

Learman grinned. "Does that mean I don't have to handle the press conferences anymore?"

The blonde agent's smile was as immediate as it was stunning. "You're officially off the hook, Detective."

Learman was wishing he were ten years younger. But he'd settle for five. . . .

The last member of the team stepped forward and introduced himself. "Jason Gideon."

By not insisting on the "supervisory special agent" title, Gideon had immediately told Learman that he considered himself a person first and not just the embodiment of a job. This ingratiated him to Learman instantly. The two men shook hands with instinctive warmth.

"Let's hope you can help," Learman said.

"You're skeptical," Gideon said, no animosity in his voice. "Why don't I ride along with you, to the latest crime scene? We can talk."

Soon, Learman — leading the way for the Tahoes — guided the Crown Vic out of the Lawrence Municipal Airport and, on the three-mile ride on Highway 24/40 from the boonies to downtown, the conversation between the detective and his guest began with an admission: "The truth is, Agent Gideon, I've never been a profiling fan."

Gideon's smile was almost shy. "You like evidence."

"Well, yes. Doesn't every cop?"

"They should. We love evidence. We just spend more time interpreting it than gathering it."

"Why a team? Why not just one of you?"

Gideon nodded, obviously considering this a reasonable question. "We each bring specific points of view and skills to this work. But with, for example, a serial killer who's in the midst of acting out, we may need to be in several places at once. Also, we're FBI agents in every sense of the word — now that we're away from the airport, we'll be strapping on our sidearms."

"In other words, you intend to pitch in."

Gideon was taking in the flat Kansas farmland as if the green field and red soil were as interesting as any case. "As much as you need us to, yes. Do you prefer Robert or Bob or Rob?"

"Rob."

"May I call you Rob?"

"Sure."

"Rob, let me tell you what we know so far." Gideon's voice was calm, even soothing.

"Okay," Learman said, eyes on the highway, assuming he would hear a recap of his own reports.

"You think of this UnSub as a monster, right?"

"Absolutely. And I hope you people are all Van Helsings."

Gideon's smile was a crinkly line. "Well, your monster doesn't look like one. He's going to look fairly average."

"How do you know that?"

"In the reports, there was no mention of attacks on homeless people."

"Right," Learman agreed.

"And the suspects show no signs of violence, other than the fatal attack itself, correct?"

Learman nodded.

"The victims, though homeless, all congregated downtown. Is there always automobile traffic in that part of Lawrence?"

"Some. Less at night, but the homeless tend to sort of stick together . . . plus, we patrol the downtown pretty thoroughly, round the clock. The city council and the mayor would throw all these indigents out of town, if they had their way."

"Well," Gideon said, "if the UnSub is not overpowering his victims with a direct attack, he . . . we'll call the killer 'he' for convenience sake, but we don't rule out a woman. . . ."

Learman took his eyes off the road, momentarily. "A woman?"

Gideon held up a hand. "He has to *lure*

his victims. He's going to be personable, able to talk to people who are by nature skittish, and yet not spook them."

That made sense to Learman. "Could he be one of them? One of the homeless?"

"Interesting thought," Gideon granted. "But probably not. The bodies have been found in different parts of the city, right?"

"Yes."

"A homeless person would have trouble moving a body around the city."

"He could have a car," Learman said.

Gideon said, "He's got his own vehicle — we don't doubt that for a second — but he has to obtain gas, to get around; and he drugs his victims, and he's got to buy the drugs somewhere, assuming he doesn't steal them. Your UnSub isn't necessarily rich, but he likely needs a steady income for this to have been going on for months."

Learman frowned. "What if he's just pretending to be homeless? Living among his prey to better play the predator?"

Half a smile dug in Gideon's cheek. "See? You're profiling already."

Learman grinned. "Yeah, guess I am, aren't I?"

And all that he'd heard made sense to Learman; already he was glad he'd called the FBI — he could see these people would at least give him a new perspective.

"All right," Learman said. "And if you have any questions —"

Farmland had given way to new housing developments.

"Let's start with this one," Gideon said. "Why did our UnSub stop for three months, then start up again?"

CHAPTER TWO

The condemned house was a run-down two-story clapboard in what had probably once been a nice neighborhood. To Special Agent Derek Morgan, this could have been a crack house in his old neighborhood in Chicago; same was true of several others along a street that brought back less than pleasant memories for a guy who had climbed from near poverty to the FBI.

Morgan was behind the wheel of one Tahoe and Hotch the other. Reid and JJ were riding with Hotch while Prentiss sat up front with Morgan. At the airport, the two Tahoes had fallen in line behind the unmarked car, a Crown Vic, driven by their skeptical host, Learman, and followed him and Gideon to this sorry neighborhood.

As they rolled up, figuring out which run-down hovel was their destination required no great deductive skills. What peeling paint remained on the structure had long since gone from white to wet-newspaper gray; the porch had separated and now leaned toward the yard as if trying to sneak away from its broken-down parent. Crime scene tape was drawn across the porch, another long strand tied to plant poles surrounding the yard, already overgrown with spring weeds. Several official CONDEMNED BY THE CITY OF LAWRENCE signs had beaten the crime scene tape to the scene by months.

A few of the neighbors stood some distance away, in yards and on sidewalks, wondering what all the fuss was about. Morgan figured violence on these streets was nothing new, but a parade of police coming to the scene probably was.

Morgan said, "Emily, when we get out, take some pictures of the onlookers, will you? Our killer might be here to see what we find out."

"Already locked and loaded," she said with a smile, holding up the small Sony digital camera she'd taken from her purse.

Several squad cars and a crime scene van were parked along the street. Conspicuous by its absence was any ambulance or coroner's van, which would have already hauled the body away.

No big deal, really, Morgan thought. The crime scene unit had no doubt taken plenty

66

of photos, and the BAU would have the chance to study the body at the morgue. Right now, Morgan and his teammates wanted their own look at the crime scene.

Uniformed officers, keeping the neighbors away, were shuffling around the perimeter, guarding the grisly contents inside, not one looking in the direction of the house itself, their focus (as it should be) on the bystanders. In addition a female officer in plainclothes and a male uniformed officer stood guard on the cracked, hole-ridden sidewalk out front. Work lights were going up — the afternoon was easing into dusk.

Learman parked, Hotchner and Morgan pulling in behind him, and soon all were out of their vehicles. While Prentiss got busy snapping digital photos of the gawkers, the rest of the team followed Learman, Gideon right behind their host.

At the curb, a trailer with a generator chugged away, the cable snaking across the yard to disappear down the side of the house.

The uniformed officer on the front walk drifted to one side as the female detective approached; she wore flat, sensible shoes and brown slacks, with a brown blazer, a tan blouse underneath. Her badge dangled at her neck and a holstered automatic bulged on her hip.

Tall and attractive, she was younger than Morgan might have expected for an officer who'd climbed the ranks to detective. Her dark hair was pulled back in a ponytail and large brown eyes peered out through black, hexagonal-shaped glasses; her nose was long, straight, chin rather pointy, her full lips could invite a lingering look from any healthy, heterosexual male, a pitfall Morgan somehow managed to avoid.

Learman said, "This is Detective Warren, my partner."

"It's Lucy," she said with a business-like smile, and was then introduced around to, and began shaking hands with, their BAU guests. They all had to speak a little louder than usual, thanks to the grunting generator.

"We can really use your help," Warren said, shaking hands with Morgan. Her voice was sweet, grip firm, skin warm and soft. "Thanks for making the trip."

"It's what we do," he said, flashing an easy smile that had been known to work wonders.

Learman said, "While I came to fetch you guys, Lucy canvassed the neighborhood."

She nodded wearily.

"How'd that go?" Morgan asked.

"About like you'd expect." Her smile stopped short of cynicism, but frustration was in good supply. "Nobody *saw* shit, nobody *heard* shit, nobody *knows* shit."

Morgan grinned. "All three monkeys."

Her cocked her head. "How's that?"

"See no evil, hear no evil, speak no evil."

She chuckled. "Absolutely. Every single monkey."

"You still did better than I would've," Learman said with an eye roll. "Around here, I usually get the door shut in my face. I figured sending a pretty girl, uh, *female detective* around might get better results."

Lucy Warren gave her partner a look.

"Hey, Luce," Learman said, hands up in surrender. "It's progress, them talking to you at all."

Gideon nodded. "Poor people in these neighborhoods are generally a fairly closed society. They don't trust anyone affiliated with the government."

"Especially cops," Learman said.

Nodding, Gideon said, "Especially cops. The fact that they *did* speak with you, Detective Warren, tells us *they're* concerned about these killings too."

"You really think so?" Warren asked. "With the rate of violent crime around here, this has their particular attention?"

"I think so. They know that if the UnSub is dumping bodies in their neighborhood, he could easily start looking for his *victims* here, too."

Behind the glasses, her eyes tightened. "So, the fact that these people will even talk to me is —"

"A sign of how scared they're becoming," Gideon finished. He gave up a good-natured grin. "You never know, Detective Warren — they might even have spoken to Detective Learman here. And he's no prettier than I am."

Everybody smiled a little; the ice had been broken.

Hotchner, who'd been watching (Morgan knew his supervisor was doing on-the-spot profiles of their new colleagues), finally got into the conversation.

"The public's aware of these crimes," Hotchner said. "What about the homeless? Has the word been gotten out to them?"

Learman shook his head. "If it has, it's not any doing of the PD. Of course, they may have seen the reports in the newspaper or on TV. There are plenty of papers around to scavenge, and the shelters have televisions."

"They deserve better," Hotchner said. His dark eyes switched to Jareau, like laser beams tracking to a new position. "JJ, work with Detective Warren to get the news out to the homeless population. They need to find shelter at night and try to stay in groups during the day. This UnSub might strike at any time."

Running a hand through curly hair, Learman said, "What's behind this thinking? Aren't you only encouraging panic? Not that I'd mind you scaring these people out of our fair city, to be somebody *else's* problem."

Morgan caught the barest flicker in Gideon's eyes that registered intense distaste for the detective's remark.

But stupid words from the local detectives they worked with tended to bounce off Hotch like bullets off Superman's chest. "The more the homeless know," Hotchner was saying, "the safer they'll be . . . but it also decreases the number of potential victims."

"Supply and demand, you mean," Learman said, getting it. "We decrease his supply, there'll be fewer opportunities for this wacko . . . and more chances for him to screw up."

With a quick nod, Hotchner returned his gaze to Jareau. "JJ, you know what to do."

Jareau said, "And I'll do it." Turning to

Detective Warren, she said, "You and I have a lot on our plate, Detective — sooner we can get started back at your station, the better."

"Ride along with me, then?" Warren asked.

Jareau smiled and nodded, and the two women left. To Morgan, it was as if the sun had slipped under a cloud and left behind a landscape as dreary as the ramshackle house that Detective Learman was gesturing toward.

"This, of course," Learman said, "is where we found Roger Rondell, our latest body."

Morgan thought: *Not "last" body, but "latest" body, an indicator of how hopeless the case must seem to Learman.*

Gideon's eyes appeared almost shut as he studied the exterior of the structure. "How far are we from the other crime scenes?"

"Factory where we found Elizabeth Hawkins is clear across town," Learman said, pointing vaguely. "Grocery store where John Doe was found is that way, too, but not as far. Junkyard is about two miles north."

Picture taking done, Prentiss rejoined them and Learman raised the crime scene tape so they could all enter the yard. The jigsaw-puzzle remains of a cement walk bisected the lawn to the sagging porch.

"Any contenders among our sightseers?"

Morgan asked.

Prentiss shook her head. "Not right off hand. Pretty much standard crime scene gawkers. Not one had 'serial killer' tattooed on their forehead."

"Shame."

Learman led the way up the sidewalk to the decaying porch and lifted the yellow tape as the others ducked and climbed the three stairs. Even though the front door was open, nobody stepped in until Learman did. This remained the detective's crime scene, and they were guests.

Without power, the house was naturally dark, spots of light visible only where the crime scene team's work lights were on, indoors and out.

Stairs to the second floor were immediately to Morgan's left, a living room yawned out to his right. The crime scene team had set up a work light near a doorway that led to an adjoining dining room, and a bright white glow cast a hard dose of reality around the dirty room, across which an electrical cord snaked its way into the dining room.

Judging by the dirt on the windows, and the smell, the place had been unoccupied for years.

"How long since anyone lived here?" Morgan asked the detective.

"Five years since anyone's been in here who was *supposed* to be," Learman said. "After that, crack house for a while, but we shut it down. Since then, the occasional homeless person has squatted, but no one has stayed very long."

Who could blame them? Morgan thought, nostrils twitching at the stench.

The furniture-free living room had ratty carpeting that reeked of urine and vomit. Windows faced the street and, on the far side, the north, provided only a filth-filtered fog that made seeing out (or in) impossible. Numbered orange evidence markers were spotted on the floor near drops of something dark, presumably blood. Near the door to the dining room, a bigger spot, a small puddle, was marked.

The BAU team was very careful where they stepped.

Members of the crime scene team — refugees from a science-fiction film in their Tyvek jump suits, complete with hoods, safety goggles and paper breathing masks — moved in and out of the house occasionally.

Learman said, "There's no place like home. But Kansas or not, don't expect me to click my damn heels together."

They just looked at him.

"*Wizard of Oz?*" Learman prodded, then shrugged. "You guys must not get out much."

Seasoned law-enforcement pro that he was, Morgan had long since stopped reacting to the gallows humor that so many cops fell into when confronted with a grisly crime scene. Of course, most cops encountered crime scenes this gruesome maybe once or twice in their careers, while the members of the BAU team routinely met such carnage.

"Have you developed an idea of what happened in here?" Gideon asked. "Was the murder committed here, or the body just dumped?"

Learman answered by waving for one of the Tyvek-suited crime scene analysts to come over. When the CSA took off his mask, goggles, and hood, he appeared to be in his mid-fifties with graying hair and bifocals that he'd kept on under the oversized goggles. His eyes were birdlike and dark, his nose long, his lips thin and more white than red.

No taller than Morgan, the CSA was slenderer, but still carried an air of strength. He smiled genially. "Wonderful day in the neighborhood," he said.

Learman said, "This is Captain Dennis

Malone, head of the Crime Scene Analysis unit."

They all shook hands as further introductions were made, then Gideon repeated his question.

"Oh," Malone said, "the crime was certainly committed here."

"Where, specifically?" Gideon asked.

Malone spread his hands. "The whole damn house. I've never seen anything like it. Blood in every room — first paint job this place has had in years."

Reid was squinting and yet his eyes seemed to pop. "*Every* room? I thought we were dealing with a *single* victim."

Shrugging, Malone said, "We are. In the basement — only one we've found so far, anyway. Could be somebody stuffed in a wall or under a floor, I suppose."

"I see," Reid said. His head tilted. "Could there have been earlier crimes? Could this have been used by the UnSub as a sort of murder house?"

"I couldn't rule that out," Malone said. "Not yet anyway . . . but the blood we found in this house is all fresh. He started in an upstairs bedroom, chased the vic around up there, then down here, through the dining room, into the kitchen, then down into the basement. That's where he finished him."

Morgan glanced back at the trail of drops across the room and the puddle near the dining room. "The UnSub chased him through the house?"

"Assuming there was one victim, yes," Malone said. "We won't know for sure until we get the tests back, to match the blood; but the blood trail, the spatter, tell the tale of a chase, yes."

Learman was frowning. "Was the killer playing some kind of *game* with his victim?"

Prentiss, frowning yet not wrinkling her brow (*How does she* do *that?* Morgan wondered), asked, "Why didn't Rondell just rush out the front door when he came down the stairs? It's right there."

"Locked," Malone said. "Back door, too. The killer set this up like a maze of locked and unlocked doors. The vic followed the path that was set up for him . . . and never had a chance."

"A *sick* game," Learman said, shaking his head.

His face blank, as if the horror were being blocked out, Gideon said, "Sick, by definition. But in practice, a power game. The UnSub was playing God."

"Power of life and death," Morgan said.

Gideon's nod was curt. His hands were rubbing together in that thoughtful way that somehow resembled washing them. "Longer the victim ran, the greater his fear . . . and the more power the UnSub felt. The Un-Sub knew he was going to kill the victim eventually, but by choosing the moment, got to feel the rush of watching the victim's hope of survival rise and fall."

"Jesus," Learman said. "This guy is fucking nuts."

Gideon cocked an eyebrow and said, "But that doesn't mean he's insane."

Learman gave the agent a slack-jawed look. "Huh?"

Half a smile formed on Gideon's cheek, digging a deep groove. "This UnSub has done everything within his ability to avoid being caught. Though some psychiatrists will argue that a sane person can't commit crimes of this type, our UnSub *knows* what he's doing is wrong . . . in the eyes of society at least. Which is why he covers his tracks." Gideon shrugged a little. "So, yes, let's grant that he's 'nuts' . . . but not necessarily criminally insane."

Hotchner held out an upraised palm as if directing traffic. "It's getting late. In order to cover more ground, we should split up."

"What configuration?" Reid asked.

"Morgan, you and Gideon stay here with Captain Malone. Detective Learman will guide Prentiss, Reid, and me to the other crime scenes."

"Good call," Gideon said.

Learman shrugged and said, "No reason why not."

Hotchner's mouth tightened into a line that was his version of a professional smile. "Fine. We'll meet back up at police headquarters."

"Law Enforcement Center," Learman corrected him. "Sound of that makes the city fathers feel safer . . . or it has till lately, anyway."

"Law Enforcement Center it is," Hotchner said.

When the others had gone, Malone ushered Morgan and Gideon up the stairs, moving carefully to avoid the orange plastic evidence A-frames. A hallway upstairs led to three bedrooms and a bathroom. The crime scene captain escorted them into the master bedroom, also bereft of furniture but with a full array of grimy windows. Perhaps twenty plastic A-frames dotted the floor.

"The first blow was struck in here," Malone said.

"You sound sure of that," Morgan said.

"I am. Blood drops are pretty round. Fell pretty straight. I think this blow took the victim by surprise. Most of the rest of the blood drops around the house splattered at an angle indicating the victim was on the move. The blood drops in this room start coming at an angle after the original spot. Once the vic realized what was going on, he took off."

Frowning, Morgan asked, "Why didn't the vic run down the stairs immediately?"

The captain led them back to the door and pointed to more A-frames on the floor of the hallway. "Before he got to the stairs, the killer got him again. The second wound slowed him down. There are fingerprints and smears on the wall — I think he was going for the stairs — but after the killer stabbed him the second time, the killer must have shoved or thrown the vic into the second bedroom, then repeated the process with the third one, then the bathroom. The victim was stabbed once in each room, then basically stumbled down the stairs to the main floor."

The captain in Tyvek led the way back down into the living room.

"The first wounds were fairly shallow," Malone said, "but the one by the dining room door, that one was deeper. . . . There's more blood."

They moved into the dining room, another bare room, this one with the expected grimy windows on one wall; now, instead of blood drops, a trail of blood made itself distinct. Another work light was set up in here, the electrical cord winding into the kitchen. The A-frames were in here marking blood spots, too.

"Have you found any evidence that *wasn't* blood?" Morgan asked.

"Fingerprints upstairs, if they don't all belong to the victim, that is. Some footprints in several rooms that don't match the victim, but some of those could be from squatters or somebody else who broke in." Malone sighed. "Bottom line though, if the killer isn't Peter Pan, we've got his footprints somewhere."

Morgan was shaking his head. "Gideon, there's something *way* off about this. . . ."

Gideon nodded as if in full agreement, but nonetheless asked, "What?"

Morgan's hands seemed to mold something in the air. "The bodies are slashed, stabbed, carved up — and that points to a disorganized UnSub. But everything else points to this guy being highly organized."

"Still in control of his hunting," Gideon said, in a voice hushed enough for church. "Yet the killings grow increasingly more frenzied." Gideon turned to Malone. "Do you concur, Captain?"

"I do. The first couple were bad enough, but nothing like this. This is a goddamn horror show."

Gideon's eyes went to slits again. "He's starting to unravel. And that means the pace of his killings is going to pick up."

"Hell," Morgan said. "You think he'll go wholesale homicidal? Are we looking at Richard Speck here?"

Gideon shook his head. "I don't know . . . but a spree of killings wouldn't surprise me. He's feeding a monster inside himself . . . but the more he feeds it, the hungrier it gets."

They went into the kitchen to find more blood, and a plastic A-frame in the left basin of the two-basin sink. That evidence marker lay next to about an inch of a pinky fingertip.

"Probably a defensive wound," Malone said. "Killer sliced it clean off."

"In a frenzy by then," Gideon said quietly.

Morgan peered out a back door that overlooked a fenced-in backyard. "Door locked?" Morgan asked.

"Locked," Malone confirmed.

"How did the UnSub and his victim get in?"

"That," Malone said, "is downstairs."

They trooped down to the basement. The

body had been removed, the outline still on the filthy cement floor in chalk. A massive pool of blood shimmered near the chalk outline.

"Damn," Morgan breathed. "The UnSub drained him."

"Slit the femoral artery," Malone said, matter-of-fact.

Morgan's eyebrows climbed. "That would do it."

"Weak as he was, he probably bled out in a relatively short time."

"How short?"

"Few minutes."

Above them, a window had been broken in, probably kicked. The windows in the basement were surprisingly good size.

"The UnSub probably forced the victim through," Morgan said.

"Or," Gideon said, "the UnSub could have seen Mr. Rondell break into this house, seeking shelter, and then followed him in."

Morgan flinched. "Into a locked, enclosed place, where he could play his sick game? But isn't that too big a coincidence? That a killer could follow a homeless person into a house that fits perfectly with his game plan?"

"The house could be a trap," Gideon said. "He watches the house. Waits for a homeless person to seek shelter."

Morgan froze. "A mouse and cheese."

"And a cat," Gideon said.

"Maybe *this* will affect your thinking," Malone said, and pointed to a small white blob on the floor.

Morgan and Gideon both squatted to see the object.

"Cotton ball," Morgan said. "What's that on it — blood?"

"Wrong color," Gideon said. "Looks more like makeup."

"Makeup?"

Shrugging, Gideon said, "Why not? He's cleaning them up, shaving them, washing them, dressing them, why not a little makeup? It's all part of the delusion."

"What delusion is that?" Malone asked.

"We don't know yet," Gideon admitted, getting to his feet, as did Morgan. "But we better find out fast. He's growing more violent, and I'm afraid it might not be long before he loses control, bypasses the care and organization he's thus far exercised, and goes straight to the killing."

"After a certain point," Morgan said glumly, "killing becomes the only thing he has. His only reality."

Malone was frowning in thought. "That

will make him easier to catch, though, right?"

Gideon shook his head, but not in disagreement. "Isn't worth the price."

"The price?"

"More people dying. Maybe quite a few more." Gideon's smile was ghastly. "We would like to catch him before that happens."

Morgan drew some breath in and let it out, a fairly risky proposition in this odorous hovel. "Are we ready to get back to the station?"

Gideon's smile was mild. "Don't you mean the Law Enforcement Center?"

"Right," Morgan said with a small laugh.

"We *should* head over," Gideon said. "I want to see what the others have found out."

"I'm not even sure I know what *we've* found out," Morgan admitted.

Gideon dropped into full professor mode. "We know our UnSub's fantasy is even more sophisticated than we thought." He pointed at the cotton ball.

"We'll test that right away," Malone said, nodding. "Let you know what it is for sure."

Back to Morgan, Gideon said, "We also know that he's devolving. There's no telling how long before there's nothing left of him but the monster, and once that happens . . ."

Morgan shook his head. "We can't let that happen."

"We can't," Gideon agreed.

On their way to the Law Enforcement Center, Hotchner called and asked them to take a detour to the morgue.

All trips to the morgue, Morgan thought, *are detours. . . .*

In the basement of the Lawrence Memorial Hospital, the city morgue bore the usual antiseptic odor and, typically, the fluorescent lighting bled color from everything, including the already pale green tile walls.

Hotchner, Prentiss, Reid and Detective Learman were waiting for them when Morgan and Gideon came in. They were in an outer room with double doors in front of them and a glass-enclosed office to their right. A sofa and a couple of chairs surrounded a coffee table that, like in any doctor's waiting room, held an array of out-of-date magazines. Lights were on in the office, but because he hadn't gotten to the window, Morgan couldn't see if anyone was within.

"Where's Malone?" Learman asked.

"Still at the house," Gideon said.

"How in the hell did you find the hospital without him?" Learman asked.

86

Morgan grinned. "We're detectives."

Detectives with GPS.

"Why are we here?" Gideon asked.

Dark-suited Hotchner, whose mortician manner was ideal for the morgue, said, "I thought it might do us some good to see the bodies up close."

Learman said, "I'll get Ken." He went over and knocked on the door of the glass office, then waved through the window.

A moment later, a slim gray-haired Asian man in green hospital scrubs came into the waiting room, bifocals on a chain around his neck.

Learman said, "This is Dr. Kenji Ohka, medical examiner."

"A pleasure," Dr. Ohka said with no trace of either sarcasm or, for that matter, an accent. Born in the United States, Morgan would guess.

After introductions all around, the doctor led them through the double doors, hitting several light switches. Fluorescents slowly flickered to life.

One wall was home to the familiar stainless steel doors of the file-cabinet-like crypt drawers with two stainless steel autopsy tables nearby, each with a sheet-covered customer. To the left of the tables, two gurneys held two more sheet-shrouded bodies.

Moving to the nearest table, Dr. Ohka drew back the sheet to the top of a dead woman's breasts. "This is Elizabeth Hawkins."

They fanned out around the table.

Morgan looked down at a petite blonde, her hair framing a serene face, the eyes closed. A thin, dark line traversed the width of her throat.

"The COD was the cutting of her throat," Ohka said, his voice as calm and quiet as if reporting the arrival of the evening newspaper on his porch.

Hotchner prompted, "There *were* other wounds though. . . ."

Ohka nodded and pulled the sheet down farther. She had been stabbed half a dozen times, although to Morgan, the blows didn't look that severe.

"The killer stabbed her repeatedly," the medical examiner said, "but not one of the blows, in and of itself, was enough to kill her."

"Superficial," Gideon said, as if to himself.

Ohka nodded. "The stab wounds indeed had little depth. As you can see here . . ." He pointed to three wounds on the left side, mid-torso. ". . . all three times the perpetrator stabbed her mid-section, he hit ribs and stopped. The same with the two blows up here . . ." He pointed to two wounds on her chest, one between her breasts, the other just above the left. ". . . when he hit her sternum and backed off. The right side blow, lacerated her appendix; but with prompt medical attention, she would have easily survived. Even the throat cutting was somewhat . . . timid. Several starts and stops, but he finally managed to accomplish his goal."

The medical examiner covered Elizabeth Hawkins with the sheet again and moved to victim number two, their John Doe. They moved to that table and again fanned out around it as Ohka lifted the sheet.

Morgan saw a tired man who looked older than the fifty-two or so his age had been estimated. His hair had grayed and he wore the pouchy face and broken blood vessels of a hardcore drunk.

"The killer used a wider blade, a bigger knife, this time — though some hesitation was still evident. He stabbed softer areas this time, but still managed to not inflict serious injury until he moved around back."

Ohka rolled the man onto his side. Rigor mortis had passed and the body had been embalmed.

"In the back, he punctured both kidneys, and this blow higher up . . ." He pointed to a wide wound halfway up the man's back on the left side. ". . . was made with greater force, breaking a rib and penetrating the heart, finally causing death."

With a lilt in his voice wrong for his words, Reid said, "He's getting angrier."

"And perfecting his craft," Gideon added.

Morgan shook his head and pointed to the neck wound. "Cutting the throat didn't kill him?"

"No," the doctor said quietly. "It was the wound in back. The throat cutting was post-mortem. An afterthought."

"Or perhaps," Reid offered, "a practice stroke for his next attack."

Dr. Ohka covered that body and moved to the gurney with the third victim. They followed again and he drew back the sheet to reveal an African-American woman: Paula Creston. Pretty and maybe, Morgan estimated, twenty-eight or so. She, too, had a wound across her throat.

"She fought back more than the others," Ohka said.

"Good for her," Prentiss said softly.

Ohka took the corpse's right wrist and lifted it. "She had defensive wounds on both hands and both arms, something the others didn't have. I suppose I should mention here that they have *all* tested positive for

Flunitrazepam, or as you probably know it, Rohypnol."

"Rondell, too?" Hotchner asked.

"His test isn't back yet. Probably fairly safe, for now, to operate on the assumption that his test will be positive, as well."

"How much of the drug?" Gideon asked.

Ohka smiled faintly, approving of the question. "That's the interesting part — the dosages are very low. Not enough to knock out a normal person, but certainly enough to make the victims — with the exception of Ms. Creston here — quite pliable."

"Was that by design?" Hotchner asked.

"Very likely," Dr. Ohka said. "The dosages were about the same in the previous three victims. I won't know about victim number four for a day or two."

Returning to the body at hand, the medical examiner said, "Again, several non-fatal stab wounds . . . but since this victim fought back, that might have been more a matter of circumstance than plan. As they struggled, the perpetrator got more and more agitated, the attack becoming wilder and wilder; but he still couldn't kill her by stabbing her. Frustrated, he slit her throat. That attack was far more savage than the others. He apparently lost control. It doesn't look as bad now as it did, when I had it opened. Actually, he came within inches of decapitating her."

The medical examiner covered the body and the group moved to the final tray and Ohka drew back the sheet on Roger Rondell.

The man was in his forties and had, truth be told, cleaned up pretty good. Morgan wondered how long the man had actually been on the street. Rondell looked far less haggard than the others.

"I've only done a preliminary exam, so far," Dr. Ohka said. "But I can tell you, even though there's more violence here than in the others, the frenzy is far more controlled — wounds made by someone who wanted to inflict pain and not immediately kill the victim."

"He wanted to see the fear," Gideon said. "He wanted to hurt this victim as a show of power. Wanted his victim to know that the UnSub, and the UnSub alone, would decide whether or not the victim would die . . . and when."

"It's apparent in his work," Dr. Ohka said, nodding. He might have been discussing an art gallery showing. "There must be a dozen wounds that would have been increasingly painful with each new strike. Finally, when he was done toying with the victim, he quickly, smoothly, severed the femoral artery. There was no hesitation this time. He had his opening for a kill, and took it."

Silence draped the somber, steel-dominated room.

Finally Learman said, "Thanks, Ken."

Learman and the ME looked toward Gideon, as if the profiler might also want to thank Ohka; but, Morgan knew, the very civilized Gideon often dispensed with social niceties when stopping a monster like this was on their "to do" list.

"We've got to catch this one quick," Gideon said. "His time frame is accelerating and he's perfecting his craft."

"That doesn't sound good," Learman said.

Gideon said, "That's because it isn't."

As they finally made their way to the Law Enforcement Center, Morgan wondered just how many more innocents would have to die before they took down this bastard. He hoped none, but the truth was, the BAU team was just getting started, and the Un-Sub? He was way out ahead of them.

Sooner or later they would track him down, of this Morgan was confident.

He only hoped it would be sooner, because later might be too late for any number of homeless people whose existence was already a living hell — a dying hell seemed too much to ask.

CHAPTER THREE

After the visit to the morgue, any preliminary discussion had been tentative and brief, both the local detectives and the BAU team having put in long days. All concerned went off to get some much needed sleep before meeting first thing in the morning at the conference room of the Lawrence Law Enforcement Center on East Eleventh Street.

Detectives Rob Learman and Lucy Warren sat on opposite sides of the table at the far end from the BAU team. Hotchner took the head of the table, as usual, with Gideon on his right and Jareau on his left. Reid and Morgan sat opposite with Prentiss settling in next to Morgan.

Though she'd had only five hours' sleep, Supervisory Special Agent Emily Prentiss felt well-rested and ready. She had never required a lot of sleep, something that had served her well as far back as pulling all-nighters as a Yale undergrad.

As the newest member of the BAU team, she was still the "new kid." She got along with all of them — they were cordial if not quite friendly, yet — though things were a bit forced with Reid, who apparently resented her replacing their previous team member, as if that were her fault. Hotch, the team leader upon whom she'd been thrust, remained reserved, but he wasn't exactly warm and fuzzy to the rest of the team, either.

Her first assignment, in St. Louis, had been much the same way, as had been her transfer to Chicago. You had to pay your dues, earn the respect. This she would do in time, and bore no grudge that she had to earn her way in. Yes, any woman faced a higher hurdle, and any reasonably attractive woman had it tougher yet; but she didn't mind. It was part of the process.

The team was, for the most part, dressed pretty much as yesterday: Hotchner wore a suit, gray today, with a white shirt and red power tie with navy blue diagonal stripes; Gideon, jeans and a pullover sweater; Reid, a short-sleeved tan shirt with a burnt-orange knit tie loosely knotted, collar button undone; Morgan, a tight black pullover, black slacks, and black athletic shoes; and

Jareau was in blue, slacks and blazer, over a white blouse, black shoes with a one-inch heel, honey blonde hair hanging free. As for Prentiss herself, she had chosen a black, short-sleeved mock turtleneck and black slacks. Her shoes were nearly twins to Jareau's, if more expensive.

The detective, Learman, wore tan slacks, a white shirt with tan pinstripes, and a solid brown tie. His partner, Warren, looked crisply professional in a burgundy blouse under a navy blue suit. Her dark hair was ponytailed back, severely, and, seated with notebook before her, wore black-framed glasses.

Short night or not, everyone around this table seemed as bright-eyed and eager to catch this killer as Prentiss.

"All right," Hotchner said, in that seemingly bland no-nonsense manner of his that masked near-obsession. "Where are we?"

Jareau spoke up first, gesturing with pen in hand. "Detective Warren and I have briefed the media."

"Good. Details?"

"We started with the late local news last night, and the TV stations have been warning the homeless to be careful and, if they can, to try to get into one of the shelters."

"Very good," Hotchner said.

Wow, Prentiss thought. *Very* good. *Hotch was effusive this morning. . . .*

"In addition," Jareau said, "both the city paper and the university paper are running this headline today."

She held up a copy of the morning newspaper with the banner: KILLER HUNTS HOMELESS.

Below that, on the left, but still above the fold (making it visible in vending machines), was a ten-point checklist of things the homeless could do to be less vulnerable.

Prentiss couldn't see the article from her chair, but she didn't need to. She knew what it said: *Get into one of the homeless shelters, don't travel alone, try to stay in public areas where there is both light and traffic,* plus half a dozen or so more suggestions, all of which sounded good in theory but flew in the face of much of what was the reality of the homeless world.

These people lived on the edges of society and a large part of how they survived was by staying invisible, and blending in. The very thing that helped them survive, day to day, as homeless citizens, was what the UnSub counted on to make them his easy targets.

"Also," Jareau added, "we've instructed the uniformed officers patrolling the area

downtown to warn any homeless they encounter . . . and Detective Warren is personally explaining the situation at the shelters,
so they can help us, too."

"That's all good," Hotchner said.

Learman said, "All due respect, aren't we
fostering panic?"

"Lesser of two evils," Hotchner said,
without looking at the detective.

Anyway, Prentiss knew, *the vast majority of
the local citizenry would not be alarmed by
the notion of a killer preying upon the homeless — the street people lived in a separate
world, and this threat was not the majority's
threat.*

Squinting as if trying to make out a distant
figure on the horizon, Reid said, "Last
night, I did some research on the clothes
the victims were wearing when they were
killed."

Prentiss knew the kid was only twenty-
five, and no one questioned his brilliance . . .
but did he ever sleep? And if he did, was it
by his heels upside down in a closet?

"In general," Reid said, with a flutter of
his right hand, "the clothes are mostly
secondhand, labels removed . . . presumably
by the UnSub. Clothes all seem to have
been in reasonably good shape, before the
UnSub attacked."

Hotchner, head cocked, stared at Reid. "You said '*mostly* secondhand.' "

"Yes. The waitress uniform worn by victim number three, Paula Creston? That was new." He raised his forefinger. "Cheap . . . but new."

Gazing down the table at Learman and Warren, Hotchner said, "I assume you've tried to track down the uniform."

Learman nodded. "Kansas City is only thirty miles up the road, and in their Yellow Pages are over fifty uniform suppliers . . . and that doesn't count all the rest of the towns within easy driving distance. Dead end."

Reid picked up again. "The clothes play some vital role in the UnSub's fantasy: the two men, both middle-aged, wore suits; the African-American victim was dressed as a waitress, a servant; and the first victim, Elizabeth Hawkins was in jeans and a blouse, very much like a soccer mom."

Hotchner said, "And what do you make of that?"

Reid's eyebrows rose above his glasses. "It's as if the Unsub is fitting them into the roles that he *thinks* they might play in society . . . if they weren't homeless."

Her mouth opened in a silent "Ah," then Prentiss said, "He's *stereotyping* them."

"Almost certainly," Reid said, nodding several times. "He's stereotyping them by age, and possibly race, but these are simple, even childish stereotypes."

Prentiss said, "This doesn't track. He's obviously smart — after all, he's a highly organized kidnapper with social skills developed enough to gain the trust of his victims."

"Yes," Reid said. "That's the dichotomy — he appears to be intelligent, yet the role-play stereotypes chosen for the victims are simple-minded, and unsophisticated."

Gideon leaned back; his hands were tented. "Maybe he's stuck." A small humorless smile formed on the rugged, sensitive face. "Maybe the UnSub's imagination will only take him so far. He has simple-minded ideas of people's stations in the social order — maybe he can't see past those."

Hotchner said, "If he can only see these people in the simplest possible terms — mom, servant, businessmen — how do we reconcile him being smooth enough to fool them all? Doesn't this make him . . . immature?"

Reid's eyes seemed to have lost focus; or was he merely focusing on something in his own mind? Prentiss was just starting to think the kid wasn't even paying attention, when out of the blue he blurted, "Or maybe just *innocent.*"

"Naive," Prentiss said, the word almost a surprise to herself, halfway out of her mouth before she realized she wasn't just thinking it.

Morgan's eyes were wide. "Maybe that's the key to how he fools them," he said with an open-hand gesture. "He *looks* innocent, naive. That's his way in, his selling point."

"He says he's lost," Gideon said.

They all turned to him.

"Maybe, he seems like a kindred spirit, another lost soul. In his way, he is, after all. So he stops and asks for directions. And they help him."

Prentiss saw them all adding that point to their list. The profile was building.

Gideon went on, talking to himself as much as to the others. "In his fantasy, he's transforming them. In his eyes, they were nothing, society's leftovers, human flotsam and jetsam. He's transformed them back into real people. Better off, at least in his eyes — an almost God-like accomplishment. He's made them better than they were in real life."

Learman had the skeptical expression of an atheist at a séance. "You think that," he said, "just because he's playing dress-up with 'em?"

This time Hotchner looked right at the detective, and his tone was respectful. "There are a lot of things that go into it, but the UnSub dressing up the victims is a very important part of his pathology."

"What makes it important?" the detective pressed. "And not just some stupid fetish?"

"His fetish is our window into his soul," Gideon said.

Learman leered. "This bastard has a *soul?*"

Hotchner stayed on point: "Consider the trouble he's going to, with these costumes. It's time-consuming, it costs him money, it increases the opportunity he'll get caught . . . it's *not* something a killer would do if he didn't have to."

Learman frowned. "You're saying he *has* to do it?"

Morgan trained his eyes on the detective. "He's done it in every case," he said. "It's odd behavior, even for someone who kills multiple times. This makes us believe it's somehow part of the fantasy he plays out in his head."

Warren, whose expression had thus far never mirrored her partner's skepticism, asked, "How does it increase the opportunity he'll get caught?"

"The first thing we'll do after this meeting," Hotchner said, "is contact every secondhand store in the area and let them know to keep an eye out for our UnSub."

Still not convinced, Learman said, "That sounds like a fool's errand, like us trying to track down that damn waitress uniform. Ladies . . . gentlemen . . . there are nearly *twenty* resale shops in the area. Goodwill, DAV, Salvation Army, the Corner Covenant, Rescue Mission, Good Shepherd, and that doesn't even begin to count the noncharitable ones. How will some yo-yo behind the counter of a resale shop even know what to *look* for?"

"Because we'll tell them," Gideon said with Job-like patience. "We're already putting together a profile. We'll give the managers and their clerks an idea of what the UnSub's behavior will be like. . . . Maybe even a physical description to some extent."

"Physical description?" Learman asked, blinking. The detective was clearly doubting his decision to bring in the BAU and their psychological crystal ball.

Seemingly oblivious to the detective's attitude, Reid cheerfully said, "Well, yes. We already know several things about him."

"Like?"

"He uses Rohypnol on the victims," the

young agent said. "That tells us he's not confident in his ability to overpower his prey."

Prentiss added, "His kills have gone from tentative to more aggressive. This suggests he's on a learning curve. He may never have killed before these murders."

"He might have a criminal record," Gideon said, "but most likely it will be a juvenile case if he does, and something far less serious than murder. Peeping Tom, perhaps, or maybe some sort of minor assault."

Frowning, looking as if he was finally buying in, Learman asked, "Bullying, maybe?"

Hotchner shook his head. "Probably not. This UnSub is uncomfortable with confrontation. Although he harbors a great deal of rage, he's just not confident enough to want to face down someone he doesn't think he has an edge on."

Gideon chimed in: "More likely, he was on the receiving end of bullying. That's part of why he's unable to confront his victims head on."

"All right," Learman said, trying to stay onboard. "What else do we know?"

"He's a novice," Prentiss said. "That means he's probably young. This fits in with the notion that he is smart but not sophisticated."

Gideon nodded somberly. "While the crimes have been well-organized, aspects point to a lack of criminal sophistication — usually a giveaway of age. This UnSub is young. He lacks the life experience to cover all the criminal bases."

Learman said, "You said he blended in with them, might look like one of them — is it possible he *is* one of them?"

"No," Gideon said, with a flat finality that even surprised Prentiss a little.

"Why not?" the detective asked.

Gideon was staring but not seeing anyone in the room; he rubbed his hands together, in that out-damn-spot fashion Prentiss had come to know so well.

His voice soft, almost hypnotic, Gideon spoke: "What he does takes time. He's got a place. It's probably isolated. The cotton swab at the abandoned house tells us he's doing at least part of his preparation right at the crime scene; but my guess is he has somewhere private he can go to."

They were all glued to Gideon.

He was saying, "The homeless wouldn't have any place private enough, surely, especially in a town like Lawrence, which is actively trying to at least monitor the street people, if not rid itself of this . . . problem."

"It's as if the UnSub is the town's Id," Prentiss heard herself say.

Hotchner shot her a look. And she knew what that look was saying to her: *Not the most politically correct thing to say, at the host's police station. . . .*

Changing the subject, Hotchner said, "A lot of those buildings downtown will have security cameras — have you checked the footage?"

"Yes," Warren said, sitting forward, her eyes bright behind the glasses. "But these people don't exactly keep regular schedules, so it's impossible to dictate when they disappeared."

"Understood," Hotchner said.

"We've had our police explorers going through tapes, but even though they spotted what *could* be our victims, now and then, they haven't come anywhere near finding anything that could be helpful."

"Get us those tapes," Hotchner said. "We'll upload them to our digital intelligence tech." To the team he said, "Maybe Garcia can enhance them and find something that's not readily apparent."

Warren nodded. "You'll have them before the end of the day."

Turning to Jareau, Hotchner said, "It's

not a lot, but let's get our preliminary profile out to the thrift stores. Young, late teens, early twenties. He'll be non-threatening and might even be one of their regulars. He'll be dressed to blend in."

"White?" Jareau asked.

Hotchner glanced at Gideon, who gave the briefest of nods.

"Probably," Hotchner said.

Turning to Detective Warren, Jareau said, "Lucy, you'll help me with this?"

"Glad to."

"Can we get someone else to help JJ?" Hotchner asked. "I'd rather Detective Warren went out in the street with us."

"No problem," Warren said. "I can get a uniform to lend JJ a hand."

"Good," Hotchner said, and formed the straight line that was his professional smile. "Thank you, Detective." Then to everyone he said: "*Someone* out there has seen our UnSub — they likely don't even know it. But we can be certain of one thing: he's spending a lot of time on those streets, trolling."

Gideon was nodding.

Hotchner went on: "He knows what he's looking for . . . even though *we're* still not sure . . . but there's something about these people that made him choose them instead

108

of other homeless people."

Gideon said, "It's possible, even probable, that the UnSub approached others."

"Yes," Hotchner said, the enthusiasm under the mask peeking out, "and our UnSub either got turned down or spooked off . . . or in some other way was forced to *not* kidnap his first choice. If we can find any of the near-misses, we'll have him."

"You sound sure of yourself," Learman said. "How can you know this perp positively had turn-downs?"

With grim patience, Hotchner said, "He's talking people into going off with him somehow. He's got to make them at ease enough for him to slip them the drugs. *Somebody,* for *some* reason, said, 'No.' Surely you've dated, Detective — I don't see a wedding ring. How many women have you asked out who've said no?"

Learman grinned. "If you're going to put that in the computer, buy more hard-drive space."

Everybody on the team, even Gideon, smiled at that.

Including Hotchner, who said, "The same thing's happening to our UnSub. Not everyone he approaches will go with him. It's our job now to find that person or those persons."

"So," Morgan said, already half out of his chair, "we're hitting the streets."

"Yes," Hotchner said, with a quiet passion that revealed how much he shared Morgan's fervor for that aspect of their job. "You go with Reid and me — Prentiss, go with Gideon. Detectives Learman and Warren will show us the most likely hangouts. JJ will take care of the thrift shops. Any questions?"

No one said anything for a long few seconds.

"All right," Hotchner said. "Our UnSub isn't letting any grass grow. Let's not, either."

Six hours later, on this lovely sunny spring morning, Prentiss stood in an alley next to a Dumpster.

Garbage smell or not, she was hungry and her feet ached, in spite (or perhaps because of) her expensive shoes.

They had not turned up a single lead so far, making it a toss-up which was going to make her heave first: the Dumpster stench or the fetid breath of the homeless guy she and Gideon were attempting to interview.

Detective Warren helped hold the man up, looking none too happy herself to be that close to their subject. The man probably had not showered since *Seinfeld* went off the air. Or maybe *Bewitched.*

Gideon gave their tentative description of the UnSub to the homeless man, who shook his head, belched, then jerked away from Warren, turned toward the wall of a nearby building on which he threw up in disgusting, dripping Technicolor.

The three law enforcement professionals stepped away from the man — giving him his privacy and dignity, of course — and deeper into the alley.

"Just why I joined the force," Warren said with a game grin, looking down to check her shoes for stray flecks. "To protect and serve."

Gideon bestowed the detective a small smile. "Most Americans are only two missed paychecks away from being like our friend here."

Warren smirked. "Minus the projectile vomiting, if I can help it."

As they moved down the alley, they spotted another person doing his or her best to stay out of sight near a Dumpster in back of a restaurant.

"Sal's Pizzeria," Detective Warren said, her voice quiet, so as not to scare the individual — a "her" — on the other side of the metal box. "Dumpster diving of choice, among our street community."

Prentiss arched an eyebrow. "That a Duncan Hines listing?"

"No," Warren said, "but I've heard all the connoisseurs recommend it."

They stayed toward the middle of the alley, Dumpster on their left, woman hiding on its far side. The afternoon heat gave the alley a foul bouquet, equal parts barf, body odor, urine and rancid food. Though Prentiss' feet still ached mightily, her appetite had vanished for some reason.

As they passed the Dumpster, Gideon held up a cautionary hand, but too late: the woman was on her feet, everything about her the scared rabbit about to bolt. Her brown eyes wide, her muscles tensed, she really seemed to think that if she froze, she would blend with the brick wall and wouldn't be seen.

The Invisible Woman she wasn't. This was a blonde fireplug in threadbare jeans, a light navy blue jacket and a black baseball cap with no lettering, her hair flying around the edge of the hat as if trying to escape.

"Hello," Gideon said gently, giving the woman an easy smile.

"Hi," the woman said back hollowly, making no effort to relax her near-flight stance.

"Could we bother you for a moment?"

Gideon asked, his voice soft. "Talk for a little while?"

She was shaking her head, but saying, "I don't know. You, you're a good-looking man."

"Thank you."

"But you can't always trust good-looking men."

"That's true. But could I ask just a few questions?"

She still seemed scared, though Gideon's manner clearly had a soothing effect. "What about, Handsome?"

"About someone," he said, "that you might have talked to."

She shrugged. "I talk to all kinds of people. I'm talking to you right now."

"Yes you are, and thank you for that." Gideon eased half a step toward her. "My name's Jason."

"They call me Ella."

He gave her a nod. "Hello, Ella. Do you have a last name?"

She favored him with a wide smile. "Not anymore. Now, I'm like Madonna. It's just Ella."

"All right, Ella it is. Ella, I'm with the FBI."

"FBI, huh? If I saw an alien, I could tell you about it, right?"

"You could. But right now we're not looking for aliens. But we are looking for someone."

"Who?"

"Well, tell you the truth, Ella." His smile
was warm. "We're not sure."

She grinned; not a pretty sight, though
once upon a time it might have been. "*That'll*
make it harder."

"Yes it will," Gideon said. "But we need
to find this person. You see, he or she is talking homeless people into going somewhere.
And when they do, Ella . . . they wind up
dead."

Ella held out her hands. "You're not saying I'm dead, are you? Well, you're wrong. I
feel fine!"

"I can tell you're alive and well," Gideon
said. "But has anyone come along and
talked to you? Talked to you about leaving
the downtown?"

"You mean besides cops?"

"Besides cops."

She sighed; her expression grew thoughtful. "Sometimes men will try to talk me into
getting into their car."

"A lot of men?" Gideon asked.

"More than one," she said, giving him a
flirtatious nod. She seemed relaxed. Safe
with her new male friend.

Prentiss wondered if the woman was delusional.

"They all want me to do a sex act with them," Ella said with a girlish grin. "They think you'll do anything just because you don't have money. I never been *that* hungry."

Gideon smiled, but he was working at it now. "Let's forget about the sexual advances, Ella. Did anyone, not looking for sex, talk to you in a way that made you feel . . . unsure of their intentions? That made you feel . . . unsafe?"

She thought about that for several long moments. "There was this one guy. *Young* guy. Wanted me to go with him. Offered me money."

"How much?" Warren asked.

"Oh, a lot! Fifty bucks!"

"To do what?" Gideon asked.

"Not sex," Ella said. "And that's what's weird. Guy didn't really say what he wanted. Usually, they can't wait to tell me what they want me to do for their measly couple of bucks, fucky or sucky."

"But this one was different?" Gideon said.

"Yeah. There was . . . something about him. Something about his eyes."

"His eyes?"

"He was . . . nervous."

"Nervous in what way?"

115

Ella considered that, then said, "He kept looking around like a little kid — you know the kind. The kind who has his hand in the cookie jar? He didn't want anybody to see us, I guess. Maybe he was ashamed being with the likes of me."

"Then he's stupid," Gideon said. "Can you describe him?"

"Sure! Should I tell you?"

"I'd rather you told an artist."

"Artist?"

"Yes. How about we sit you down with an artist, and he draws a picture of who you saw?"

Ella smiled at him. "What's it pay?"

Gideon took his wallet from a pocket and a bill from the wallet. He held up a crisp new portrait of Benjamin Franklin before her amazed eyes.

Prentiss knew this was not Gideon spending FBI money — they weren't authorized for this kind of thing. This was him buying the woman a bowl of soup; well, a hundred bowls of soup, more or less.

Her eyes glittered with the treasures of Ali Baba's cave. "All I gotta do is sit with an artist while he draws this creep?"

"That's all."

"Where at?"

Gideon looked at the restaurant's rear

door. "This place open?"

"Yeah, they have a lunch crowd." She checked her watch. "Should be pretty much cleared out by now."

"Right here, then," Gideon said, shrugging, pointing to the pizzeria. "I'm buying . . . and you'll still get this when the artist is done."

He meant the hundred-dollar bill.

"You're a lot different than that nervous kid," Ella said. "You know how to treat a lady. Jason, you got yourself a deal."

"Thanks, Ella," he said, and they shook hands.

Prentiss admired Gideon for all of this, but was glad she wasn't the one shaking that particular hand.

Turning to Warren, Gideon asked, "Can you get a forensic artist down here? If not, the FBI in Kansas City can —"

"We've got a guy," Warren cut in. She got her cell phone from her pocket. "Have him here within half an hour."

At a rear table, Gideon talked quietly with Ella as they split a half-cheese, half-pepperoni, the thin woman eating far more than Gideon. At a nearby table, Prentiss and Warren shared a small veggie pizza that Prentiss found delicious, despite her knowledge of the Dumpster and the alley a mere wall away.

Midway into the meal, the artist arrived, a tall, crewcut uniformed officer about forty-five. His nameplate read FLETCHER, and he carried a sketch pad under an arm.

Ella informed Officer Fletcher that he couldn't have any of their pizza and Bruce gave her a smile and told her he'd already eaten lunch, so that was okay.

Ninety minutes later, Ella strode out of Sal's Pizzeria with her hundred-dollar bill tucked in a shoe, and the BAU team had a drawing that gave them some idea what their UnSub might look like.

He wasn't anything special.

Young, blond hair down to his shoulders, under a blue baseball cap he wore backward. Wide-set eyes, straight nose, full lips. No scars, tattoos, or birthmarks that Ella had noticed.

She and the UnSub had spoken weeks ago, about when Paula Creston had gone missing, so it was anybody's guess how accurate this drawing was by now.

Still, the UnSub staring up at them looked like half the KU student body. If he didn't make a mistake — and no one saw this drawing, and called the police — this guy was so unassuming, he could kill for years before anyone caught him.

But that, Prentiss thought, *was before Hotch and Gideon had brought their team of profilers to town.*

And, new kid or not, Prentiss was proud to be part of helping take an evil predator like this one off the street.

Twenty-four hours and this one's turning out to be all right.

At first, all the fat fuck could think about was eating. We fed him, slipped him a little dessert in his dessert, and then he was fine.

Once he was easier to handle, we got him back to the place, cleaned him up, but he whined through the whole damn thing, even with the roofies! Thought we were going to just have to do him right then and there, the fat fuck. He starts crying like a little girl.

We didn't like it.

Look, asswipe, you're only in this position because you're a fucking loser, so take the hit. If you were strong enough, you'd kick our ass and get your *ass free. But you aren't, you can't, you're a pussy, and we're going to have it our way.*

We'll let him sleep through the night, dose him again, then tomorrow, when the light's just right? We'll do our work. We think he'll be good — guy's a natural. He might be the best one, so far.

Waiting for the light is the hardest part.

CHAPTER FOUR

With afternoon giving way to evening, the BAU team and the Lawrence detectives returned to the Law Enforcement Center to look into other possible leads while JJ Jareau went about releasing the composite forensic drawing to the media.

Dr. Spencer Reid didn't seem to have any hobbies — his interest areas appeared too broad for such a narrowing down. His co-workers knew little about his personal life; oh, they knew he liked to read (at a speed they found dizzying), and that he had a keen interest in physics. But none of them — except maybe Gideon — was aware of his interest in jazz.

Reid had learned a little about this form of American music when he was younger, but lost the time required for serious listening when he enrolled at Quantico. Not long ago, Reid had reestablished his friendship with Ethan Hyde, a tall, dark-haired, bearded musician who had himself once sought a career with the FBI — in fact, started at Quantico at the same time as Reid.

But Ethan quit after just one day of training.

In the midst of a case on the post-Katrina streets of New Orleans, Reid and Ethan had bumped back into each other. At the time Reid was suffering a crisis of confidence, having endured captivity in the hands of an UnSub the team had been tracking. With Ethan's help (and Ethan's music), Reid had found his bearings again.

Since then, jazz had been a way for Reid to keep himself grounded. Today, his mp3 player's earbuds nourished him with "So What" from Miles Davis' *Kind Of Blue* album. He particularly liked Miles' inspired riffing in the confident context of what Cannonball Adderly and John Coltrane brought to the mix. Recorded nearly fifty years ago, the album still sounded as if it might have come out yesterday.

Now, sitting behind a desk in a strange police station in Lawrence, Kansas, Reid found a certain peace, thanks to Miles and the band. He was reviewing reports of homeless people who had been reported missing over the last six months. Just as he'd anticipated when Hotch gave him the assignment, very few were on record.

A mere three, to be precise . . . and none matched any of the victims. That was not unusual, however: homeless people seldom had anyone in the straight world who might miss them, meaning no one to report a disappearance.

The first missing-persons write-up told of the disappearance of Kenneth Bream, mentally ill, twenty-five, a Lawrence resident who had been on the street for just over two years. His sister, Karen, found him every week or so, and tried to help him along; but Kenneth generally resisted such aid and only occasionally accepted food or money from her. Then, a month ago, Bream had disappeared completely. No one had seen him since, and he hadn't appeared at any of his usual haunts thereafter. Karen had reported him missing within a week, but the Lawrence PD had no luck locating him.

Though he might be a victim of this killer, Bream might also have wandered off anywhere. A homeless individual needed no one's permission to relocate, in Bream's case to seek escape from his sister's well-meaning help and maybe hop a freight or hitch a ride or even scrape up bus fare and start over on the streets of some city friendlier to his breed than Lawrence.

The only thing Reid knew for certain was that Bream was far too young to be their John Doe.

The next missing person was a sixteen-year-old girl whose family had been put on the street after the father lost his job and they were unable to meet their mortgage. The parents, Glenn and Bonnie Howell, had reported going to sleep one night in their '95 Toyota (their only remaining possession of note) and waking the next morning to find their daughter gone. Normally, they slept in front and Amy slept in the backseat. Neither parent heard a sound overnight.

Again, a possible victim, but nothing that matched up with the killer's known victims. Amy Howell remained still missing, but more likely a runaway than an abduction victim.

The third candidate, Frank Webster, was fifty-three and had no criminal record. He'd been reported missing by another homeless person, Bennie Salazar, a homeless Gulf War vet in his forties; but they couldn't identify Webster without Salazar, and now no one could find him, either. This didn't necessarily indicate any foul play had taken either man, not in the limbo world of the homeless.

Hotchner came in, his suit still immaculate even after a day in the warm spring weather interviewing street people; though Reid had helped solve his share of mysteries as a profiler, the young agent had no idea how his supervisor managed such feats.

Hotchner asked, "Any luck with the old reports?"

Shaking his head and pulling out his earbuds, Reid said, "I don't see anything that might help us understand this UnSub much less find him."

Briefly, Reid summed up the three missing persons.

Hotchner nodded, then drew up a chair, across from Reid. "Gideon thinks you're doing well. Back on your game. Do you agree?"

Chagrined that Hotch had brought up what he saw as his weakness, Reid nonetheless resisted the urge to turn away, forcing himself to maintain eye contact.

Without looking down, he paused the mp3 player. "Yes. I'm fine."

"Good," Hotch said. "We were worried about you for a while there."

"I was worried, too. I appreciate your concern. I won't let you down."

"That never occurred to me," Hotchner said with a rare smile. "What do you make of this case?"

Reid frowned in momentary thought. "Clearly, this UnSub is a schizophrenic."

"Interesting. How so?"

"Look at the dichotomies."

"Such as?"

"Such as he's able to talk his victims into going with him, but he can't face the idea of killing them, if they're not drugged."

Hotchner's nod was barely perceptible, but his narrowed eyes said the supervisor was right with the young agent.

Reid continued: "Usually, an UnSub — too unconfident to kill without having an edge over his victims — will not lack the confidence to face them down, which is of course necessary to kidnap them. He would catch them alone, unaware, and overpower them."

Hotchner was getting it. "But *our* UnSub doesn't drug his victims until *after* he's made contact."

"Yes, and not just contact, but a connection." Reid felt the rush of intellectual excitement that accompanied a profile coming into focus. "And he's careful. He's capable of blending in, and works hard at not getting caught. Yet he discards the bodies where they can be easily found. Granted, an abandoned factory, a grocery store

Dumpster, a junkyard, and an abandoned house, are not exactly dropping the bodies in the town square . . . but he's got to know they're going to be found. And he doesn't seem to mind."

Raising an eyebrow, Hotchner said, "That could be because he's careful not to leave any DNA *or* fingerprints."

"Possibly," Reid said. "But the crime scenes seem picked for some reason beyond simple isolation, something we haven't discerned yet."

Hotchner nodded. "That's all well-observed and well-reasoned. Keep at it."

"Thank you. I will."

A slight tilt of his head meant Hotchner was changing subjects. "Have you checked in with Garcia, to see if she's had any luck with John Doe's fingerprints?"

Reid shook his head and admitted, "Haven't talked to her. Sorry. I've been burrowed in with these files."

"Understandable. But make time, and give her a call."

"Yes."

Hotchner granted the younger agent yet another smile. "I'd say you're back on your game."

Reid grinned. "Thanks. I agree."

Hotchner rose and strolled off. As he

watched the team leader go, Reid replaced his earbuds and hit PLAY. On the mp3 player, the second cut, "Freddie Freeloader," took off with the blues-based piano of Wynton Kelly taking the early lead. Behind him, the understated bass of Paul Chambers and the rock steady beat of Jimmy Cobb gave Kelly space to weave in and out without being intrusive. Then in came Miles, and the song shifted into a whole new gear. Reid closed his eyes and listened, letting the music carry him into a dark, airy space.

He knew onlookers would think he was wasting time, but what he was really doing was clearing his head so he could think about the crime scenes. The BAU team had missed something, he just knew it. These sites were not chosen randomly or picked exclusively for their sequestered nature. Somehow the locations themselves were part of whatever fantasy drove this monster.

By clearing his mind, Reid gave himself space in which to roll the problem around, examining it like a Rubik's cube, studying each side, every facet, every possibility.

He was, in fact, barely cognizant of it when the next song, "Blue in Green," began.

He wondered if it was possible that the UnSub was trying to create a family. But something didn't click with that analysis — although the killer had assigned roles (both men in business suits as father figures, the mother in the factory, the sister in the waitress uniform), the crime scene settings themselves jarred.

Why put the businessmen in a house, and behind a grocery store? Why put the waitress in a junkyard, or the possible maternal figure in a factory? None of this made any sense, even in the "sense" of a delusional mind. Or was the killer *reversing* roles — father at home or near a grocery, mother at work in a factory. . . . What was the UnSub trying to tell them?

He put them where they would be found.

Was he trying to tell society that he was performing a service? That he was leaving these people better off than he'd found them? Or maybe — hideous as it was to contemplate — maybe the UnSub was planning his defense ahead of time, in case he got caught.

A jury would see the grieving families of the victims, but the UnSub — at least in his mind — could counter with, "Look what I did for them, I cleaned them up, I made them better than they had been."

In essence, the killer might be saying he cared more for the victims than their own families had.

"Reid!"

Startled, he pulled out the earbuds as his eyelids rolled back and he was looking up at Hotch, who was back suddenly.

"We're meeting in the conference room," his supervisor said. "I think you're onto something about the crime scenes. We're going to dig into it."

"Great," Reid said, but truthfully? Reid didn't know if he was onto anything or not. The more he thought about his less-than-a-theory, the less sense it made. No solid colors had taken shape in the Rubik's cube in his mind.

Reid got to his feet, grabbed his sports jacket off the chair. Hotchner was studying him like a bug on a slide.

"What were you doing just now?"

Flushed, Reid said, "Thinking. Trying to make sense of the crime scenes. What Sherlock Holmes called ratiocination."

Hotchner's eyebrows went up. "Really? Is that what it's called?"

Was that sarcasm? A joke? Another sign of Hotchner's legendary if largely missing-in-action sense of humor? It was spotted from time to time, like Bigfoot. . . .

Reid followed Hotch into the conference room. The rest of the team, but for Jareau, was already there; and Learman had taken his customary seat at the far end of the table. The attractive female detective, Warren, was not present.

Reid sat in his usual seat as well, across from Morgan.

They all looked expectantly at Hotchner, in his leader's position at the head of the table, his eyes swiftly scanning a file. After a moment, he closed it, tossed it on the table, and looked around at those present, seeking and briefly holding the eyes of each.

"We've been proceeding, so far," Hotchner said, "as if the crime scenes are chosen first and foremost for their isolation, following the logical notion that the UnSub needs privacy for his ritual, and seeks to escape detection during its commission. Not ruling out that factor entirely, Reid has been considering another possibility."

As one, they all turned toward him and Reid found himself squarely on the spot.

He would have to wait until later to figure out whether Hotch was testing him or showing faith in him. Right now, nothing remained but to plow ahead.

"If you'll forgive me," Reid said, "I have to begin with things we all know. Just to refresh our memories and provide context."

Several nods around the table granted

Reid this.

"Recently, when we were in nearby Kansas City, Charles Holcombe killed homeless people in a meat packing plant he'd inherited. Though he turned the plant into his personal house of horrors, it was, at heart, a crime scene of both isolation and convenience."

More nods around the table — even Learman, who had no doubt seen news coverage of the crimes just up the road, and probably had friends there who kept him informed of what had taken place.

"*These* crime scenes, however — although at least somewhat isolated — seem to lack the element of convenience. They are in different parts of the city, with no discernible pattern to their selection. *Why* did our UnSub choose these four places?"

Gideon sat forward, eyes slitted but glittering with thought and possibility. "You think they somehow are part of his pathology?"

Reid's gesture was almost casual, as if he were reading off the ingredients of a recipe; in a way perhaps he was.

"Gacy, Gein, Dahmer," he said. "They all used their own homes for the commission of their atrocities — in the case of Dahmer, a cramped apartment with other tenants in the building. Gein and Gacy had seemingly more freedom, since they owned their own homes."

"Excuse me," Prentiss said, her head titled, her eyes alert, "but didn't Gacy live in a normally well-populated neighborhood, while Gein was in the country, a farm-house?"

"Yes," Reid granted. "Still, they shared a certain privacy. Gacy threw some victims in the Des Plaines River, but nearly three *dozen* were buried in the crawl space below his house. This UnSub has stayed basically invisible, and doing that has taken real work, real effort, real thought . . . so why increase his chances of being caught by bouncing around, crime scene to crime scene?"

Eyebrows up, Morgan said, "Maybe he thinks the different crime scenes make him harder to track."

Nodding, Reid said, "A genuine possibility. Without discounting that, though, wouldn't it make more sense to have one place, a safe place, where he could do his work?"

"You're asking an insane person to make sense?" Learman asked.

Gideon fielded that one. "This is a highly organized individual. You've been on the job for years, Detective Learman — you know that most people aren't organized enough to kill one person and not foul something up. This UnSub has killed at least four people, not leaving enough evidence behind to give us even a *hint* as to who he is. As soon as you think his illness makes him less competent, you give him an overwhelming advantage."

"This UnSub is very smart," Reid said, his eyes first on Learman but then moving from teammate to teammate. "Which only makes it more probable that he's picking these places because they have some sort of resonance, either with himself or the victims."

Learman's skepticism seemed to have faded. "Any idea what that resonance is?"

Reid shook his head. "It's there, but I just don't have enough pieces to put it together."

Hotchner said, "We need more data — you can't make bricks without clay."

Reid wondered how many of his fellow BAU teammates realized Hotch was paraphrasing Sherlock Holmes, and wondered, too, if this was a direct, droll reference to his own ratiocination remark.

Gideon was saying, "We'll get Garcia on it right away. Maybe she can track down a connection between the crime scenes."

Hotchner gave Reid a look with a bland surface but an accusatory subtext. "Have you called her about the fingerprints yet?"

The young man shook his head. "No. I didn't get to that — I was working on this theory."

"Call her."

Reid excused himself and stepped out into the hall; he got his cell out and hit speed dial.

Garcia answered on the third ring. "Reid! How is lovely rural Kansas?"

"Not that rural. Not that lovely, either."

"I sense you come seeking knowledge, Grasshopper."

"I do."

He found a chair and sat and explained in detail to her about the four crime scenes, giving her all the relevant information. He needed no notes to do this.

"I'll work my magic," she assured him. "Any other feats of legerdemain I can do for you?"

"Just one. Hotch wants to know if you had any luck with John Doe's fingerprints."

"Sometimes the magic works, sometimes it doesn't — tell him not yet. No matches anywhere."

"That's all right," Reid said. "I may have another route for you to follow, anyway."

"Really? Do tell."

"There's a missing homeless man here named Frank Webster. He's about the right age. He was reported gone by a man named Bernie Salazar, probably Bernard. Now he's also disappeared."

"Got it," she said, her chirpy cheerfulness putting him in a better mood.

"Thanks, Garcia."

"Keep the phone close."

"Will do."

Back in the conference room, he reported the phone call, editing out the fun and games.

"So," Learman said, his face as drawn as a college kid who'd pulled one too many all-nighters. "What do we do while we're waiting for your computer guru to save our bacon?"

Hotchner glanced at his watch. "We get some sleep. We can't work twenty-four hour days without compromising our ability to perform. Garcia will call if she finds something, and I've put JJ on the hot line — she'll alert us if someone calls about the drawing. Then, in the morning, if we still don't have —"

He stopped as Detective Warren came into the conference room, her face pale as death, a plastic evidence bag containing a piece of paper in her right hand. Reid's first thought was that the PD had found another body.

Instead, Detective Warren said, "SSA Hotchner, I know you're here to help us with this serial killer, but I was wondering if you and your people could spare enough time to take at least a preliminary look at another case."

Hotchner's eyebrows went up and his jaw went down. Finally he said, "We *are* busy here, Detective Warren. . . ."

"I know, I know; but there's been a kidnapping. And *that's* FBI business."

Hotchner frowned. "Are you sure it's a kidnapping?"

Warren held up the bag. "This is the ransom note."

Hotchner accepted the note, which he read through the plastic. When he finished, he cocked his head and gave her a wary look. "You're sure this is *real?* It seems absurd on the face of it."

"The parents in the case don't feel that way. They haven't seen their daughter since yesterday."

"Hotch," Gideon said gently. "Share with the rest of the class."

Hotchner drew in a deep breath, then exhaled, and his expression went beyond grave into grim. The bagged note now rested on the table in front of the supervisor.

Who said, "Not only are we looking for a serial killer in Lawrence, Kansas, this community also seems to boast a kidnapper who is demanding a ransom of . . ." He checked the note. ". . . precisely sixty-eight thousand dollars."

"*Sixty-eight* thousand?" Morgan asked, his stunned expression including a grin that Reid realized was inappropriate but justifiable. "What kind of figure is that for a kidnapper to ask for?"

Gideon said, very quickly, "A specific amount an individual is attempting to raise." The senior agent sent his gaze to Detective Warren. "You know the family?"

"We do," Warren said, finding an empty chair at the table and sitting. "Gerry and Patti Bonder. I've known Patti since high school. Their daughter Kathy is a good girl."

That phrase struck Reid as intrinsically Midwestern: *good girl.*

Warren was saying, "If she's ever late, Kathy phones her folks . . . but not last night. They're frantic. Out of their minds. You can understand. . . ."

"Yes," Gideon said. "How old is Kathy?"

"Twenty."

Hotchner looked at Gideon and Gideon

nodded back — the exchange lasted only a second, but spoke volumes about the relationship between the two supervisory agents.

Then Hotchner said, "All right — here's what we'll do. Jason, you and Prentiss see if you can help Detective Warren with the kidnapping. The rest of us will stay on the first UnSub."

Gideon's eyes met Warren's. "Would you say this family is well-off? Wealthy?"

Warren frowned. "Well-off, maybe. Wealthy is overstating it. Gerry owns a successful restaurant, Patti teaches school. They're certainly not rich."

Reid said, "But far from poor."

Gideon said, "This may explain the relatively small ransom."

A thought crossed Reid's mind and he felt his mouth tighten and his chin crinkle, as he warred with himself about whether to let it out.

Noticing this, Hotchner gave him a sharp look. "What's on your mind, Reid?"

Reid swallowed. "The odds of a serial killer, and a kidnapper, both in action at the same time, in a town this size? Astronomically against."

Frowning, his expression almost alarmed, Morgan said, "You can't be serious — you think *this* is our guy? It doesn't fit anything we know about the UnSub!"

"No way to be sure of that without more data," Reid said. *Can't make bricks . . .*

"Reid," Morgan said, "get serious. A girl from a well-off family is hardly homeless."

Reid shrugged, gestured with open hands, fingers wiggling. "He could be changing his targets, and even his technique. After all, our UnSub has already defined himself a kidnapper, and a skilled one."

Detective Learman had the expression of an over-worked air traffic controller. "They *do* that, these psycho killers of yours? Change their M.O. willy-nilly?"

Ignoring Learman's over-the-top characterization, Gideon said, "As the UnSub hones his skills, he might be looking for a greater challenge."

"You can't *know* this is the same perp," Learman said, with a scowl.

"We can't," Reid admitted. "But it could be. Our UnSub may be evolving. All of us start out not knowing how to do something, and then the more you do it, the better you get, the more refined your skills."

Prentiss said to Learman, "This UnSub probably began with small animals as a child."

Reid nodded. "Parents often mistake the

killing and dissecting of animals by their child as an avid interest in science, instead of an early warning sign of a potential pathology."

"One-third of the homicidal triad," Gideon said softly.

Learman blurted, "What? What kind of bullshit —"

But Detective Warren cut him off with a hand as she said, "I've heard of that, Agent Gideon; but I don't really know what it is."

Gideon glanced at Reid, deferentially.

Reid said, "There are three behaviors that are seen as early signs of potential homicidal sociopathy: cruelty to animals, as we've already discussed; enuresis — that is, bedwetting — beyond the age of twelve to fifteen . . . some experts differ on the exact age; and pyromania."

"Is this a theory," Learman asked, "or science?"

"I would call it a scientific theory," Reid said. "Interviews with, and research into, the early lives of serial killers have borne the triad out."

Gideon said, "Our UnSub almost certainly displayed one or, more likely, all of these behaviors before moving on."

Learman frowned. "Moving on to what?"

"To killing people."

Warren was sitting forward, eyes sharp behind her glasses. "So, now you think he might be upping the ante — homeless people aren't enough of a challenge. But this is kind of fast, isn't it? After only four vics?"

Gideon said, "Sometimes it *is* fast . . . but what is at least equally likely is that he's killed more than four times."

Both detectives looked a little sick, hearing this.

Gideon went on: "Four is just how many bodies we've found. Charles Holcombe, in Kansas City, murdered over sixty people . . . and we never found more than a few pieces of over three-quarters of them."

Glumly Morgan said, "And that the UnSub's victims have been among the homeless complicates it further."

Reid said, "In 2005, nationally, the number of homeless grew by twelve percent — this was followed by a nine percent rise last year, yet the homeless population of Lawrence has been relatively static."

Gideon, nodding, said to the detectives, "Your city might be an anomaly — it happens. Or . . . you could have a problem that you were unaware of, until you started finding bodies."

Learman and Warren traded a concerned glance.

Hotchner said, "In no way does this conversation mean this *is* the same UnSub, understand. But we do have to consider that possibility."

Gideon looked at his partner in the kidnapping investigation, Emily Prentiss. He smiled reassuringly. "Let's take this one step at a time. We'll keep an open mind, and treat this as a disconnected kidnapping that merely happened to happen in a jurisdiction where we were already at work."

"Agreed," Prentiss said with a crisp nod.

Hotchner stood. "Fine, but anyway you parse it the stakes are going up," he said. "And we're being spread thin. Let's stay alert, and keep open to possibilities . . . and Gideon? Keep in touch."

Gideon nodded. To Learman he said, "May I make the call to the Kansas City FBI for tech support? I'd like to limit their involvement, until we determine whether this is one case or two."

Hotchner glanced at Learman, who said, "No objection. I admit I'm impressed, hearing you people talk."

"Thank you," Gideon said.

"Now," Learman said, rising, "impress me with some action. Some results?"

No one on the team responded. More talk was not what the detective was after.

■ ■ ■ ■

Bengie Gray awoke, terrified and shivering.

He lay face down on a piece of carpeting that smelled of urine and shit, and the odor made him want to puke. He was naked except for his tightie-whities, and a shiver ran through him as he realized he had no idea where he was, how he got there, or what was going on. His feet were free but his hands were cuffed behind his back, cold steel cutting into the flesh of his wrists.

The darkness was nearly complete.

He could see small windows on a nearby wall, but they were covered with heavy dark drapes, only the barest amount of light leaking around the edges. His instinct was to scream for help. He hesitated, though, wondering who would come, if he called out. Might be help . . . or might be whoever had done this to him.

Better to stay quiet, till he knew more of what he was up against.

He rolled onto his side, then managed to get his knees under him, and rise that far. He tried to rise further and, *damn,* tipped over.

He started again, and again, and on the fourth try, he finally managed to get to his feet. His stomach roiled, lurched into his throat, and he clamped his mouth shut to keep from throwing up.

Forcing himself to breathe through his nose, he finally got his stomach to settle down and he began tentatively exploring his surroundings.

The room was long, narrow, and devoid of furniture. *A trailer,* he thought. His only company seemed to be the ratty carpeting. Moving slowly, still feeling sluggish and hungover from whatever they'd doped him with, he eased forward.

A half-wall with a counter and sink separated this room from a tiny kitchen. In there, a refrigerator sat in the corner, its door hanging open, which told Bengie, *No electricity.*

He would kill for a drink of water, but no way could he work the faucet with his hands cuffed, assuming there *was* water. . . .

Hoisting his ass onto the counter to try to turn the faucet on was just out of the question, as would be opening any of the cabinets over the sink and above where a stove should have sat next to the fridge.

Standing, Bengie listened harder than he ever had in any class at KU. *Maybe,* he thought, *if I paid this much attention in class, I wouldn't be in this shit.*

He heard nothing.

Nothing. Not a bird, not a bug, no wind, no nothing. Bengie Gray had been homeless for months now, but never in his life had he felt this alone. He was somebody's prisoner, that much he knew. What they had in mind, he had no idea, but he could guess, and words and images . . . *rape, torture, murder* . . . made his stomach roil again.

He had to get out.

He had to get out now.

At the far end of the trailer was a hall, but Bengie wanted no part of going deeper into this white-trash hellhole. He could see a door on the wall opposite the end of the half-wall, and, although he figured it for locked, he could only try. . . .

Backing to the door, he finally managed to get his hands on the knob and twist. Knob moved a quarter of an inch, and held.

Locked.

He tried again, same result. Door was definitely locked, but did move slightly. How good could the lock *be?*

Panic rising in him, Bengie made his plan. He moved into the living room area, only a foot to the right of the half-wall; because of its placement, he would have to hit the door at an angle, but it was worth the try.

He had to try.

Breathing through his mouth rapidly in and out, firing himself up as he had seen football players do before games, he sprinted forward, dropping his shoulder and yelling in rage as he hit the door.

The yell turned to a scream as pain shot through his shoulder and into his neck, and down his back to send an electric burn through every fiber of his being.

The next second, though, he rejoiced as the door swung open with a nasty crack as something in the frame broke. His exhilaration lasted for exactly one second as he traveled on through the door, realizing he was three feet in the air with no stairs below. Gravity and momentum tipped him forward, the ground rushing up to meet him.

The first thing to hit was his nose, which smashed back into his face with a sickening crunch and another burst of pain. The rest of him hit the dirt hard, the air whooshing from his lungs.

Sprawled there, breathing blood through his nose, he struggled to turn his head and open his mouth as he coughed and spit up.

He couldn't even scream now.

Get up, his mind urged, but his body didn't seem to hear. Tears rolled down his cheeks and he finally got his breathing under control, still spitting blood occasionally, as he made another attempt to rise.

No luck.

Then, from behind him, he felt himself being hoisted to his feet.

Was this his captor, or help?

Panic again swept over him and, as soon as his feet were under him, Bengie whipped around to see a kid about his own age. He ran the face through his memory bank, but he came back empty.

The guy smiled.

Bengie tried to smile back, every cell of his body burning with pain.

"Where you think *you're* goin', Fuck-face?"

A fist flew toward him, smacked straight into his chin.

After an instant of blazing white light, accompanied by sharp, equally blinding pain, a blissful blackness swallowed him.

CHAPTER FIVE

Next to the passenger side window, Supervisory Special Agent Jason Gideon sat with Detective Warren, Prentiss and Jareau in the backseat, as they drove through some nice neighborhoods on the twenty-minute ride to the Bonder home.

Even though darkness had settled over Lawrence, Gideon could easily make out the large, two-story brick structure with its three-car garage in a neighborhood full of such homes, its street number — 714 — well-lighted above a mail slot.

Upscale if somewhat cookie-cutter, the Bonder home informed one and all that the family living there had money — but kidnappers usually struck families whose homes screamed *big* money, at least when ransom was the primary motive, as seemed the case here.

Still too early to tell, he told himself as Detective Warren eased her unmarked Ford

Crown Victoria to a stop in front of the home and killed the lights.

They were expected.

Before leaving the Law Enforcement Center, Gideon had contacted the Kansas City field office and spoken to an agent the team had worked with on the recent Holcombe case. SA Morris Parker was a no-nonsense field agent who had been on the job for twenty years. Parker had promised to have a tech team on its way to Lawrence to monitor the Bonders' phones within the hour.

The ransom note had been typed on a computer, the printer obviously an inkjet, and trying to track the origin of the note was part of the procedure. The original had been sent to the Lawrence crime lab while a duplicate lay in Gideon's lap. There was no need to read it again — the note had been short and succinct.

IF YOU EVER WANT TO SEE YOUR DAUGHTER AGAIN, PAY $68,000. IN-STRUCTIONS WILL FOLLOW. NO COPS!!

The stoop was just big enough to hold Detective Warren and her BAU contingency. Her ring of the bell elicited the outside light coming on, and the door swung open to reveal a tall middle-aged man with slightly graying hair, parted on the left and combed over, his sky-blue eyes rimmed red. He wore a pink dress shirt with a loosened black tie, top button undone, black suit pants and black loafers.

"Mr. Bonder," Warren said with a business-like smile. "These officers are with the FBI."

His eyes looked a little glassy as he studied Gideon. The man seemed to be searching for an appropriate response to that, but was having no luck.

"Jason Gideon, Mr. Bonder. We're sorry for your trouble." Gideon extended his hand.

Bonder took it, shook it.

"Thank you for coming," Bonder said mechanically.

The phrase had an odd ring — as if the FBI group were party guests — but Gideon knew all too well the tortured mental state this parent was suffering.

Knowing ritual could be comforting, Gideon introduced the rest of the crew, individually, and Bonder shook all of their hands and even managed a smile, pained though it was.

Then everything froze, there on the stoop, as if the missing girl's father had exhausted his social repertoire.

His expression gentle, Gideon asked, "May we come in, sir?"

The distraught father shook, said, "Sorry . . . certainly . . . sorry . . . please," and stepped aside and gestured them in.

They stood in an entryway with a Mexican tile floor; a small table on the right held a vase of fresh flowers. To the left, stairs rose. A hallway went back to the kitchen and great room, to the right a formal dining room, Bonder's black suit coat hanging on the back of the nearest chair.

Immediately to their left, a set of French doors standing half-open, looked onto a formal living room, into which Bonder led them.

The room was smaller than Gideon might have thought, judging by the outside of the structure. Immediately to his left heavy curtains concealed a picture window. The wall opposite him was home to a low-slung beige sofa on which an attractive if brittle-looking middle-aged woman perched, her slender frame in a light brown v-neck sweater and tan slacks, her slippered feet barely touching the deep-pile carpet.

"This is Kathy's mother," Bonder said. "Patti."

She made no effort to move off the sofa.

Her wavy blonde hair cascaded over her shoulders, and full lips were set in a firm frown while red-rimmed dark blue eyes had gone puffy from crying.

"Darling," Bonder said gently, "these are FBI agents, here to help us."

Mrs. Bonder squinted at them, as if noting their presence for the first time; she had the same shock-numbed demeanor her husband had displayed at the door.

"I'm sorry," Bonder said to Gideon, working up that awful smile again. "You'll have to forgive me — I've forgotten your names already. The wheels just aren't turning yet."

"I understand," Gideon said, taking a few steps toward the wife and holding out his hand over a mahogany coffee table. "I'm Jason Gideon."

The wife sat forward a few inches to give him a weak handshake.

Gideon introduced Warren, Prentiss and Jareau, briefly, and Mrs. Bonder acknowledged the group with a single nod.

Straight-back armchairs sat at right angles to the sofa, creating a straight line with the coffee table to divide the room almost in half. On the wall with the French doors were two large sets of mahogany shelves filled with hardcover bestsellers. Behind the armchair at the left end of the couch, more

French doors led into the great room, where a big wall-mounted wide-screen television was the obvious focal point.

No television in the living room, Gideon noted.

Gideon understood why the room of comfort and family had been rejected in favor of this colder, more formal area: unconsciously, the Bonders were attempting to separate themselves from any reminder of their daughter and the normal family life that had been disrupted.

Mrs. Bonder suddenly sat up straighter. She tried to brighten, though it didn't really work. "I don't mean to be rude. Won't you please sit down?"

Warren and Jareau remained standing as Gideon and Prentiss each took a chair, the former choosing one close to Mrs. Bonder.

The husband came over and sat next to his wife and they joined hands, an automatic action that made Gideon feel a little better. These two people drew strength from each other, a gift from God in this trying time. . . .

After allowing the couple a few moments, Gideon said, "I'm sorry to have to ask this, Mr. Bonder, but could you accompany Agent Prentiss to your kitchen, please? She has a few questions for you."

Bonder looked from his wife to Gideon.

"Any questions you have for us, Agent Gideon, you can ask right here."

"Actually, sir, we can't." Gideon gave the couple the kindest smile he could muster.

Their host was shaking his head in confusion.

Gideon gave it to him straight: "We need to interview you separately."

Bonder frowned, the pieces clicking together quickly, the shock no longer dulling him. "Are you saying we're *suspects?*"

"No, sir. I'm saying protocol requires that we interview you separately. Together you may influence each other's responses, and we can get a clearer picture of —"

"You *are* saying we're suspects." Bitterness edged Bonder's lips. "Our daughter's been kidnapped and *we're* suspects? *That's* your idea of finding out what happened to Kathy?"

Gideon considered the man seated before him.

Gerald Bonder was a successful businessman, a man used to getting things his way — who might bull ahead when cornered, as he obviously felt now. Gideon knew the most expedient thing might be to bull right back, but decided on a different tack.

Bonder was on his feet now, his wife next to him looking terrified. "Are you *listening* to me, Gideon?"

"I am indeed," Gideon said, his voice barely above a whisper. "But now you need to listen to me, sir. The longer you remain an obstacle to my team moving forward, the more you accomplish two undesirable things: You keep us from looking for your daughter, and you make me wonder why."

Whether it was the low volume of Gideon's words — or their high impact — that froze Bonder, the agent couldn't know. But freeze Bonder did.

"I have no desire to make this situation worse for you," Gideon said. "I'm a parent. I understand. But you need to make your first priority helping us in our effort to return your daughter safely to you. And that includes full cooperation. Are you ready to do that, sir?"

The response came not from Bonder but his wife: "*Yes!* We're ready — anything! Gerry, please do whatever these people ask. You said it yourself — they're here to help."

Gideon kept his voice low and calm. "Thank you, Mrs. Bonder. . . . Sir? Are you ready to go to the kitchen with Agent Prentiss, so we can begin?"

Bonder nodded. "Yes. Yes, of course."

Rising, Prentiss turned to Jareau. "JJ, would you come with us?"

"Certainly," Jareau said, and gave brief business-like smiles and nods to their host and hostess.

"Mr. Bonder," Prentiss asked, "could you show us into the kitchen, please?"

The restaurateur looked at her numbly for a second, then, zombielike, led the two agents out the way they'd come in, leaving Gideon and Detective Warren with Mrs. Bonder.

For her part, Detective Warren stood quietly in the corner observing. Nothing had been said, but she clearly was comfortable deferring to Gideon for the interview with the victim's mother.

Mrs. Bonder was sitting forward, her eyes earnest. "I'm so sorry about the way my husband behaved, Mr. Gideon. Gerry's not used to . . ."

Powerlessness, Gideon thought.

". . . to not, you know, being able to *control* a situation."

But Gideon waved off the apology. "He's a devoted father who's worried about his daughter. Anyone would react similarly in his position."

Relief relaxed her. "Thank you . . . thank you for understanding."

"Thank you for yours, Mrs. Bonder. Kathy — she's your only child?"

Mrs. Bonder nodded and her mouth tightened and her chin crinkled. She was squeezing a tissue in her hand, a box of them next to her on the sofa.

"We were both career-oriented," she said. "Gerry and I decided, early on in our marriage, that we'd rather have one child and do it right than . . . anyway, Kathy has been a joy, a perfect child. We couldn't have dreamed for better, not the way the world is these days. But now *this* nightmare . . ."

"Start at the beginning," Gideon prompted.

The woman composed herself and raised her eyes to meet Gideon's — somewhere within her, she'd understood that she and her husband were suspects, and for the good of her child, she would get that notion out of the way, get it dispelled.

And the clarity of her red-tinged gaze went a long way toward doing that, where Gideon was concerned.

"I got home from school about 3:30 yesterday afternoon," she said. "I teach high school English at George Washington Carver. Kathy doesn't usually get home until nine or ten o'clock, at the earliest. She's in the film and drama school at KU."

Gideon gave her another comforting smile. "Does she want to be a filmmaker?"

"No, though she loves film. She knows more about the movies of my lifetime than I do. . . . No, she wants to be an actress. She had leads in school plays from grade school on. She was the Baker's Wife in *Into the Woods,* her senior year."

"Sondheim," Gideon said with an appreciative nod. "Vocally challenging. She sings, as well?"

"Oh, yes. She has a wonderful future. . . ." Hearing her own words, Mrs. Bonder swallowed and got herself another tissue, dried her eyes, blew her nose.

"What with rehearsals for plays and so on, Kathy's always getting home late. Even though she's a college student, she's living at home, so we do insist she keep in touch. She always calls me after her last class, which gets out around four. I settled in to grade some papers yesterday and waited for her to call . . ." She shook her head. ". . . but it never came."

"Was that unusual?"

"It's the first day she's *ever* missed a call."

"She has a cell phone?"

"Of course. But when I tried calling her, the phone went right to voice mail. I left a message for her to call me."

"You tried several times, I assume?"

"More than several times, Mr. Gideon —

I tried again and again. Seven or eight times. I'm sure the phone company could give you that information. Gerry called her several times, too."

Gideon cocked his head. "And you never got more than voice mail?"

"Never once."

Gideon nodded. "Could I see a photo of Kathy?"

"I gave one to the detective already," Mrs. Bonder said, gesturing to Warren on the sidelines.

"I just need to see one myself," Gideon said with a shrug and a smile meant to soothe. "A recent one, if possible."

Mrs. Bonder went to the shelves, selected a bound leather volume, and returned to the sofa. Flipping through photo album pages, she soon found the shot she wanted.

"This is from Easter weekend," Mrs. Bonder said.

She handed Gideon the photo.

Kathy Bonder was a pretty girl — Gideon knew that such a phrase was considered politically incorrect these days, and Kathy was, after all, twenty. But he knew a pretty girl when he saw one, and Kathy fit the bill, her shoulder-length hair nearly as blonde as her mother's, though she had her father's light blue eyes.

In the Easter photo, Kathy wore a flowered dress, posed with her mother, in a floral dress as well, the two looking like sisters.

"She's lovely," Gideon said.

"Thank you. That was a good day."

Gideon's head tilted. "This was Easter, last year?"

"No — *this* year. Just a few weeks ago."

Interesting — a few weeks ago, and already Mrs. Bonder had carefully filed the photo away in a precious leather-bound book.

"When did you receive the ransom note?"

Mrs. Bonder let out a long breath. Her eyes tightened. "This morning. Tucked in the rubber band around the morning paper."

Gideon glanced over at Detective Warren.

"The only prints on the paper belong to the Bonders and their paper carrier," Warren said quietly. "No prints on the note. And we've canvassed the neighborhood — no one saw anyone or anything out of the ordinary."

Gideon nodded the detective his thanks, then returned his attention to the kidnapped girl's mother. "Does Kathy have a boyfriend? Anybody she's serious about?"

She shook her head. "Not really. She was very focused on film school and, in particular, her acting. She *did* date, but it certainly

160

wasn't the center of her life. There have been a couple of young men. . . . I gave those names to Detective Warren when she was here, earlier."

Warren said to Gideon, "We're still running them down."

Attention back to Mrs. Bonder, Gideon asked, "Was Kathy having trouble at school, perhaps, or maybe at a job?"

Mrs. Bonder shook her head. "School was Kathy's full-time job, as far as we were concerned."

"Maybe she wasn't getting along with someone at the college. Director of a play, or a co-star?"

"No, she gets along just fine at school — at least as far as we know. There aren't parent-teacher conferences at KU, like high school days. And she isn't in a play right now."

Warren injected, "We'll talk to her friends and teachers tomorrow."

Gideon nodded his assent to that. Then to Mrs. Bonder, he said, "How about trouble for your husband — anyone angry with him? Or with you, for that matter?"

She considered the question, then said, "No one I can think of."

"Disgruntled student from Carver, maybe . . . or an unhappy employee or former employee of your husband's?"

"No. No one comes to mind."

"Does the amount the note demands hold any significance to you or your family? Sixty-eighty thousand dollars?"

"No. It does seem . . . a strange figure."

"Is it a figure you could raise?"

"Yes."

"Wouldn't be the amount that's in a certain savings or checking account . . . ?"

"No."

"And you haven't heard from the kidnappers since the note?"

She shook her head, obviously again on the verge of tears.

"Not hearing yet has no special significance," Gideon assured her. "These things have no set time table."

Mrs. Bonder nodded, but seemed unconvinced as she helped herself to another tissue.

Before Gideon could ask another question, the doorbell rang.

Mrs. Bonder rose automatically, as did Gideon. He noticed Detective Warren's hand now hung loosely near her hip-holstered gun.

Gideon was expecting the FBI tech team, but the idea of a very brazen kidnapper coming to the door could not be dismissed entirely. Hadn't the ransom note been delivered to the Bonder doorstep?

Mrs. Bonder led the way through the French doors, Detective Warren next, her hand now touching the butt of her pistol, Gideon bringing up the rear.

Prentiss, Jareau, and Mr. Bonder came down the hallway from the kitchen, all with eyes alert. As Mr. Bonder moved toward the door, Prentiss stood her ground in the middle of the hall and Detective Warren subtly edged between Mrs. Bonder and the door.

Nerves were naturally on edge and the law enforcement team was being overly cautious; but if they were going to err, let it be on the safe side.

Still looking shaken, Mr. Bonder opened the door onto Morris Parker and a slew of other agents.

"It's okay," Gideon said quietly, stepping up alongside Bonder.

Prentiss and Warren both relaxed visibly.

"FBI, Mr. Bonder," Parker announced, showing his ID. "I'm Special Agent Morris Parker. May we come in?"

"Yes, yes, please," Bonder said, more self-assured than before. Evidently, Prentiss had taken him to a better place; later, Gideon would ask her about it.

Parker entered, another agent slipping in behind him, while Jareau made the introductions, and hands were shaken all around.

Tall and rangy, Parker — bald but for a monklike wreath of light brown hair — had wide-set brown eyes, a straight nose and a doughy if pointed chin. He wore a white shirt under a navy blue blazer with a muffled navy and maroon tie and dark gray slacks, the blazer cut well enough to almost hide the bulge of the pistol on his hip.

Almost.

Next to Parker stood a familiar-looking agent Gideon couldn't quite find in his mental Rolodex.

"This is my partner," Parker said with a gesture, "Jeff Minet."

Gideon remembered the thirty-ish agent now — from Alabama, Minet had a Good Ol' Boy accent he could turn on and off at will. Blond and blue-eyed, darn near a poster child for the Aryan Nation, Minet was (Gideon recalled) nearly as tenacious as he was smart, and he was plenty smart. Gideon wondered if the young man might not be BAU material himself one day.

A small army of agents — carrying boxes and/or cases of equipment and wiring — trooped into the house and, without waiting for permission, swept past the group standing in the entryway. Two went upstairs, three went into the dining room, two went through the French doors into the living room and three more straight back to the kitchen.

While Jareau directed the techs as to where to unload and set up, Gideon, Prentiss, and Warren stepped outside to confer with Parker and Minet. Away from the family, the closed door between the agents and the Bonders, the agents compared notes.

With neither preamble nor malice, Parker simply asked, "Are they in on it?"

Gideon's eyes went to Prentiss, who gave him a curt head shake and a twitch of her red-lipsticked mouth, which summed up meant her interview with Mr. Bonder had gone much the same way as Gideon's with Mrs. Bonder.

"No," Gideon said. "We believe this is the real deal."

"All right," Parker said, asking for no details about how the profilers had reached their conclusion. "How do you want to play this?"

"They haven't heard from the kidnappers yet," Gideon said. He glanced at his watch. "And it's getting late."

"Significance of that being . . . ?"

"Being, if I am a kidnapper and want to

terrify this family, I call in the middle of the night."

Parker nodded. "So, you want us all here, all night."

"Yes. Your team is trained to handle the phone monitoring — we'll let them do it. If you don't hear from the kidnapper later tonight, then my people and I will be at the university, first thing in the morning, to talk to Kathy's friends and teachers, and to see if we can re-create her day."

Minet said, "Y'all want us to pick up the security videos from the college, or you plan to take care of that yourselfs?"

Detective Warren reminded all concerned whose turf this was. "Our crime scene unit got to the security office at KU today," she said. "We have people going through the security videos already."

"Sounds like everybody's got something to do," Parker said, with no jockeying or posturing. "We've got the family, then. And we'll call if anything happens before morning. Anything else?"

Gideon pondered for a moment. "Let's talk about that ransom note."

"Okay."

"Nothing special in it, except the amount of the ransom. Doesn't make sense. Even if he grabbed this young woman at random, the kidnapper still delivered the note, personally, to the house. He would have seen that there was more money than he asked for. Why not just add a zero or two?"

Minet said, "Sixty-eight thousand is a damned odd figure *with* or *without* an extry zero."

"This job is supposed to be about logic," Gideon said, eyes widening. "It's about understanding what is behind the behaviors of our UnSubs."

"That's not exactly a news flash, Gideon," Parker said dryly.

Gideon ignored the remark, saying, "The thing is . . . I've got no idea why the kidnapper asked for this particular amount. Emily?"

Prentiss shrugged. "Makes no sense, unless it's some kind of prank . . . and if it's a prank, where's the girl?"

Gideon frowned. "These people have more money than $68,000, though Mrs. Bonder can think of no special significance for that amount — it's not their savings or checking balance, for example." He looked at Prentiss. "Did Mr. Bonder fire anyone lately who might make that yearly salary?"

"No," Prentiss said. "And I went down that road with him. I remembered that oddity on the Jon-Benet case."

Parker asked, "What oddity is that?"

Gideon said, "The ransom demand was the same amount as a recent bonus the child's father had received. This cock-eyed figure *does* have a significance . . . and we need to find out what it is."

And, for the next half-minute or so, they just stood there in the dark, listening to crickets.

Finally Gideon said, "I've got a bad feeling." He gestured at the Kansas FBI agents with a professorial forefinger. "You talk to this guy tonight, be careful."

"We will," Minet said, his Southern accent practically gone.

"Are you the negotiator, Jeff?"

"Yes, sir."

"Experienced?"

"Yes, sir. Don't worry — I'm not going to let this bastard harm the girl."

Gideon gave the younger agent a world-weary smile. "You may not have anything to say about it."

Prentiss, her pale skin like ivory in the moonlight, the red of her lipstick looking almost black, said, "We do know *one* thing about this UnSub."

They all turned to her.

She said, "Anybody only asking $68,000 ransom for a beautiful young girl from a

168

well-off family? Clearly *doesn't* place much value on human life."

No one could argue with that.

Then they went back inside and laid out their scenario to the Bonders. The phones were tapped, recorders set up, techs either settling in or saddling up, depending on whether they were part of the team running the equipment.

The Bonders sat limply in the living room, holding hands like the shattered sweethearts they were, while the agents and Detective Warren moved into the dining room to confer one last time.

As Gideon, Prentiss and the detective were preparing to leave, a technician in an FBI windbreaker approached. A young African-American in his mid-twenties, he said, "Kathy Bonder's cell phone was turned off yesterday afternoon, around one o'clock. She was on campus then."

"How do you know?" Gideon asked.

"When the phone is turned on, it 'talks' to the nearest cell tower. Kathy Bonder's phone last contacted a tower at 1:04, yesterday afternoon. It was then turned off . . . and has *stayed* off since."

"Can you track her phone now?"

The tech shook his head. "Not while it's turned off."

Parker posed a question that badly needed asking: "Is it possible Kathy Bonder's in on this herself?"

Gideon shrugged. "Minus the ransom note, the explanation for her phone could be as simple as she turned it off herself, before a class started. I do need to talk to the parents again, though. Together, this time."

The quintet returned to the living room, the others trailing behind Gideon. Mr. and Mrs. Bonder, on the sofa, showed the strain of the last twenty-four hours.

"I know this has been a difficult time for you," Gideon said, "and we'll do our best to help you through it . . . but I do have to ask a few more questions."

"Fine," Mr. Bonder said. He seemed shell-shocked, no fight left in him.

"This is the hardest question to ask, under the circumstances, but it has to be. Is there any way your daughter could be involved in this?"

Mr. Bonder's expression darkened, while his wife paled, her mouth dropping open.

"Well, she *is* involved, isn't she?" Mr. Bonder said acidly. "She's the fucking victim."

"Gerry . . ." Resting a hand on her husband's knee. Mrs. Bonder said, "That's not what Mr. Gideon meant."

"I know what he meant. He wonders if our daughter is capable of extorting money from her own parents."

"I wish she *were*," Mrs. Bonder blurted. "Then she'd be safe, we'd *know* she's safe. . . ."

"It's silly," Bonder said, his spine back. "We've always given Kathy everything she wanted, our *full* support. . . ."

"Mr. Bonder," Gideon said, "Kathy is twenty and living with her parents. Attending college for most young people means getting out from under the parental thumb, usually leaving mom and dad behind, moving away to some new city and having adult responsibilities. However loving, you may seem, forgive me, a burden to your daughter."

Bonder flushed with anger. "A *burden?*"

Gideon held up a hand and said, "If you think about it, you'll understand why I have to ask. You've told us Kathy's an actress, a gifted one. We have to make sure this isn't a role she's playing, in an attempt to break free of parental control."

Bonder took a deep breath, let it out, and finally nodded. "I do understand. But it's not that way."

Understandably defensive, Mrs. Bonder

171

said, "We've always had a wonderful relationship with our daughter. We've supported her in everything's she's done, and she's returned our love and support by always being honest, always telling us what's on her mind, what's going on in her life. If she's wanted or needed money, we've given it to her."

But her husband had a dazed expression. Like Gideon, Bonder seemed to know that he and his wife might easily be viewed as smothering parents.

Gideon changed the subject. "Would you have any idea why Kathy might have turned her cell phone off, yesterday afternoon?"

"Do you know *when* she turned it off?" Mrs. Bonder asked.

"Just after one p.m."

"Acting class," Mrs. Bonder said without hesitation. "The instructor is adamant about turning cell phones off during class."

"What about after?"

"Acting class ended at 2:30, then she had a film class at three. She would call me every day after the film class, and usually she would get something to eat before rehearsal, if she was in a production."

"And you say she isn't in a play right now?"

"No," Mrs. Bonder said. "The school year

is winding down — only a couple weeks until finals."

Gideon said, "Thank you, Mrs. Bonder — Mr. Bonder. I know how difficult this is for you, and it gives me no pleasure making it more so."

Bonder nodded, but Mrs. Bonder barely seemed to have heard Gideon.

Who said to them, "Try to get some rest, if you can. Special Agent Jareau will stay with you, if you need anything." He gave Jareau a quick glance and she nodded. They had already moved a Lawrence PD officer onto the hotline JJ had been tending.

Jareau said to the Bonders, "I can answer any questions you might have about why, or how, we're doing certain things, as we resolve this. And if any media comes around, part of my job is to handle that."

Bonder said to Gideon, "Agent Prentiss told me that the kidnapper would be likely to call late tonight."

"I agree with her assessment," Gideon said. "But that doesn't mean he will absolutely call tonight. There are no real absolutes in these situations."

"I see," Bonder said numbly.

"As I said before, you and Mrs. Bonder need to try to get some rest. If you stay up all night waiting for a call that doesn't come, you'll be weaker and less alert tomorrow, when it does. The longer this goes on, if we allow it to sap our energy and spirit, the more the advantage will shift to the kidnapper."

Both Bonders nodded.

Of all the hard things Gideon had had to say tonight, what he said next was the hardest: "We'll do everything in our power to get your daughter back, but you have to realize . . . this is just the beginning."

CHAPTER SIX

When he awoke, Bengie Gray felt strange — as if his mind had roused before his body, which was just this thick unresponsive shape he was trapped inside.

Something was wrong, terribly wrong — he couldn't move, he could barely think. His eyelids weighed a ton and — even when he did manage to force them open — he couldn't see much.

He was back in the dark trailer, his nose and eyes puffy from his fall, his jaw aching from the battering. The tiny lines of light around the drapes were brighter now.

Must be day, he told himself.

But he had no idea *what* day, or whether this was morning or afternoon. . . .

His hands were still cuffed behind him. He tried to bend his knees to get them under him again, but when he did, something tugged at his ankle. He pulled again, but whatever-it-was wouldn't let go. Keeping his eyes open was an effort, but he did, looking down through the gloomy light to see something metallic around one ankle, and the other, too.

He was shackled to something!

He couldn't see what. . . .

With an oddly calm, detached resignation, Bengie realized he was going to die here. He wanted to fight, to get up and run, but his brain was so fuzzy, like somebody had stuffed cotton balls inside his head, and just to stay awake was all he could do. . . .

The creak of a door opening startled him, and he again made the herculean effort of lifting his eyelids to peer back under his own arm to see someone silhouetted in the doorway, the outside world bright behind him, but not blindingly so. Dusk? Anyway, this was the door he'd broken, in his escape attempt.

Bengie began to cry as the shape in the doorway moved closer to him; but he was also watching himself cry, in some isolated part of his mind, noting his tears clinically. In the ugly gray light, and with his screwed-up vision, Bengie couldn't tell anything about the person except that he or she was dressed in dark clothing.

"You awake, Superstar?"

Bengie said nothing. He didn't recognize

the voice. This wasn't the voice that had called him "Fuck-face," was it? Or was just the tone different?

His captor kicked him in the side and, even through his logy haze, Bengie felt the jolt of pain.

"Wake up — we've got work to do."

Trying to make out his captor through puffy eyes, Bengie finally realized the guy was wearing a stocking mask. Also a dark long-sleeved shirt and dark slacks. While Bengie lay there like a lump, the captor knelt and undid the shackles, freeing the prisoner's legs — not that Bengie could make them do anything, much.

His side burned from the kick and — even with the incredible heaviness he felt throughout his body — the urge to hurl came over him again. He repressed it.

The captor yanked the handcuffs, jerking Bengie to his knees and making him cry out in pain.

"Get up! Time is money."

What did that *mean?*

Bengie wanted to drop to the floor and just curl up in a ball; but the thought of his captor yanking on the cuffs again encouraged Bengie instead to slowly rise to his feet.

"Put those on."

Bengie looked sluggishly around, but

didn't see his clothes anywhere. A small pile of apparel lay neatly folded on the floor — not his things, though. His brain might have gone fuzzy, but he knew he could recognize his own clothes.

"Those . . . aren't mine," Bengie muttered.

His captor slapped Bengie, hard, cheek stinging like fire and the pain from the jarring of his broken nose shooting lightning bolts from every follicle in his head to every cell in the bottoms of his feet. Tears sprang from his eyes and trailed down his cheeks.

"Get *dressed,* I told you," the captor said, unlocking the handcuffs.

Once the metal had slipped off, Bengie brought his hands around and began rubbing his wrists. They hurt, but having the cuffs off was sweet respite. His shoulders ached from his arms being pinned behind him for so long. He rolled his shoulders, trying to ease the stiffness.

The captor raised his hand and Bengie flinched.

The captor laughed and said, "Get dressed. The light's right, we've got to get to work."

"The light?" Bengie asked. "What light?"

"Magic hour. Just shut up and get dressed and do as you're directed."

Supervisory Special Agent Aaron Hotchner and the team were back at it early in the morning.

Losing Gideon and Prentiss to the kidnapping investigation had been a blow, but the BAU team had to do what they could to assist on both cases. And if Reid was right, and these were somehow one case, the profilers would be well-positioned.

On the other hand, that left three of them — Morgan, Reid and Hotchner himself — to do the work of five.

As for Jareau, she was tied up with her own duties as liaison with the Lawrence PD. In that capacity, she now had two cases instead of one. And Hotchner tried not to even think about Gideon and Prentiss trying to cover for the whole team on that kidnapping.

Back in the conference room, the trio of profilers had spread themselves around the table. Detective Learman and Jareau were off somewhere else in the Law Enforcement Center, and Detective Warren was with Gideon and Prentiss.

That left Morgan to work up a geographical profile of the city, to see if he could find a pattern and possibly anticipate the next crime scene; while Reid was still looking for another connection between the victims, other than homelessness — maybe, in some fashion as yet undetected, the victims had the crime scenes in common.

Hotchner agreed with Reid that the scenes of the crime were important to the UnSub for a reason other than simple isolation. But right now that belief — and the familiar frustration of sensing something just beyond his fingertips, no matter how hard, how far, he reached — was about all Hotchner had.

His current tack was to search back through crime scene photos, for any hint they might have missed. They were pretty close to having what they thought was an accurate profile of this UnSub, but Reid's doubts about the crime scenes had kept Hotchner from delivering that profile to Learman.

After all, whatever was driving this UnSub to pick these particular places could be a key part of the profile.

The pictures Hotchner studied now were from the junkyard, a crime scene the team had not visited, and needed to get more familiar with. Paula Creston, the African-American victim, had been found there by one of the yard employees.

The UnSub had cut a hole in a Cyclone fence to gain entry, then — judging from the photos and the plastic A-frame evidence markers — had chased the victim around the junkyard, stabbing her with a knife, but with her slipping away and the chase resuming . . . until finally they got to a spot near the office, where the killer finally delivered the coup de grace of cutting her throat.

Hotchner studied the close-ups of the blood spots on dirt paths weaving through the junkyard. The UnSub would chase her for a short distance, then there would be a number of blood drops all in one place, after which the chase would begin anew, move to another spot and so on. This happened at least four times before she was finally allowed to die near the office.

Paula Creston had defensive wounds on both arms and her hands. She had fought back, but with the Rohypnol in her system, had simply not been strong enough to escape.

The photos told him several things about the case. Rondell, the fourth victim, had been chased through the abandoned house, as well. The first two, Elizabeth Hawkins and John Doe, had been relatively stationary kills. The last two had both involved the killer toying with his victims. The UnSub was becoming more confident on this level too.

This gave Hotchner a thought.

"Who's got the autopsy reports?" he asked.

The other two both shuffled through the piles of paper on the table.

"Right here," Morgan said.

"Check the Rohypnol levels on each of the victims."

"The first victim showed a dosage of five milligrams," Morgan said. "Same for the second. The third and fourth were both around three milligrams. What's normal?"

Reid said, "One to two milligrams for a person below one hundred ten pounds, two to four over. How much did Elizabeth Hawkins weigh?"

Morgan checked the chart. "One twenty-one. The UnSub gave her over twice the normal dosage for her size."

"No wonder it was a stationery kill," Hotchner said. "She couldn't have run."

"The dosage is going down, though," Reid said.

"To give him a greater challenge," Hotchner said.

"And another level of confidence," Morgan said. "This UnSub is devolving fast. At this rate, he won't even be using the drugs, before long."

"Becoming a killing machine," Reid said.

Hotchner studied the photos again. This crime scene photographer was either the most thorough he had ever seen . . . or the rawest rookie ever.

The photographer had taken pictures of everything — stacked cars, a stray wheel, paths that crisscrossed the junkyard. These included several shots that might prove helpful: the blood drops; a footprint with a ruler in it (for scale); and, near the footprint, a small divot on the path.

Hotchner frowned at that latter photo.

Providing neither prompting nor hint, he passed the photo to Reid. "Look at this, then show it to Morgan."

As the other two men eyeballed the photo, Hotchner went through more crime scene shots and finally found another that included the small distinctive hole in the earth; and then he found two more.

"What do you see?" Hotchner asked.

"A footprint," Reid said.

"And that's all you see?"

Reid got the point and tried again, studying the photo. But when he glanced up again, he remained confused. He passed the photo to Morgan, pointing out the hole in the earth.

Reid asked Morgan, "What *is* that?"

Morgan scrutinized the photo, then shrugged. His eyes went to Reid, then to Hotchner. "Some kind of indentation. It's at an *angle*. . . ."

Hotchner stood and arranged the photos until they overlapped and formed one image of three different identical marks in the dirt comprising a triangle, each divot about two feet from the others.

"A camera tripod?" Reid asked.

Frowning, Morgan said, "Is the son of a bitch recording his kills?"

Pointing at the photos, Hotchner said, "That's a lot of work for *one* UnSub. He's got to break into the junkyard, deal with his drugged victim, set up the camera, make sure she runs past it, then catch her at just the right moment, so he can have his scene where he stabs her multiple times . . . then she runs off again. But how can he chase her and follow the action with his camera, all at the same time?"

Reid said, "He has a partner."

"*Two* UnSubs," Morgan said gravely.

Hotchner sat, nodding. "This changes the profile," he said.

Getting out his cell phone, Hotchner hit the number for Jareau and she answered on the second ring. "Is Detective Learman with you?"

"Yes. We were just about to —"

He cut in. "I need you both in the conference room, immediately. We have something."

In less than a minute, the blonde agent and the skeptical detective bounded into the room, finding Hotchner in the process of searching through the pile of crime scene photos.

"What do you have?" Jareau asked.

But Hotchner did not answer her question, instead demanding of Learman: "Who took these?"

Hotchner was indicating the photos on the table of the indentations in the dirt.

"Be an ID number on the back," Learman said with a *what's-the-big-deal* shrug. "Why?"

Hotchner flipped a photo. "Who is number 3?"

Learman frowned in confusion. "Murphy. Harold Murphy. He's one of four civilian crime scene analysts we employ. Why — what did he do?"

Indicating the arrangement of three overlapping photos, Hotchner said, "I think he just gave us an important clue," and briefly explained their significance as he saw it.

Then Hotchner said, "We need to talk to Mr. Murphy. Is he available?"

Learman seemed puzzled. "Not in-house, but it's easy enough for me to get him in here."

"Do so."

Twenty minutes later, photographer Murphy stood before them — young, tall, gangly, with blond hair and Coke-bottle glasses, he looked more like the center on a JV basketball team than a crime scene analyst.

After a round of introductions, Murphy asked cheerfully, "What can I do to help? It's this homeless killer, right?"

Hotchner ignored the question but posed his own, indicating the three arrayed photos on the nearby table. "What do you make of this? And why did you take the trouble to make a record?"

Murphy, squinting down at the photos, answered almost immediately. "Looked like the feet of a tripod, to me. So I shot 'em."

"Why did tripod marks seem significant to you?"

He shrugged. "I thought maybe they meant the killer might have videotaped or filmed the murder."

"Did you mention it to anyone? Your supervisor?"

Murphy paled. "No. I guess I figured they'd look at the photos and see for themselves."

Hotchner's mouth twitched; it wasn't a smile. "Photos aren't three-dimensional. Your observation as a photographer, and a crime scene analyst, was important. You should have called it to everyone's attention."

"Yeah. I . . . I guess I should have."

Hotchner couldn't waste time taking this kid to the woodshed. "Well, you learned something today. And you did preserve some important visual evidence. Did you photograph the other murder scenes?"

Murphy shook his head. "Not all of them. The factory and the alley behind the grocery store, I made those shots; then this, the junkyard. Somebody else did the house — Stacy Perez, I think."

"Did you notice these tripod marks at the other crime scenes?"

Pushing his glasses up on his nose, Murphy said, "In the factory, you'd think there'd be similar impressions in the dust, but I couldn't find any. Lots of footprints, several types of tennis shoes and the victim's sandals — kids were always sneaking in that place to goof around. But no tripod marks."

"Maybe there *was* no tripod at the factory," Hotchner said. "The killer could have had an accomplice who recorded the murder with a handheld camera."

"Yeah, that makes sense . . . if you can say *anything* makes sense about any of this tragedy."

Hotchner nodded. "And you didn't find any marks at the second scene because the alley's concrete? Any scratchings?"

The young crime scene analyst shook his head. "No, but anyway, I figure that body was just dumped there. I don't think we've found that murder scene yet."

Hotchner shot a look at Learman.

Learman shrugged. "There's not enough evidence to say either way. It was the cleanest crime scene, in terms of blood trails and the like; but there was blood in the Dumpster. Vic could have been killed *in* the Dumpster . . . or somewhere else and dumped."

"You've looked for another site?"

"Of course. But we've found nothing, and anyway, where would you *look?*"

Hotchner arched an eyebrow. "The other crime scenes maybe?"

Learman shook his head. "John Doe's blood hasn't shown up at any of the other crime scenes, so he wasn't killed there, either."

Hotchner nodded to the young crime scene analyst. "Thanks for your help, Mr. Murphy," the profiler said. "Next time?"

"Yes, sir?"

"You spot something you think is evidence at a crime scene, don't just shoot it — point it out."

"Yes, sir," Murphy nodded, properly chagrined, and left.

Hotchner played host, gesturing to the conference table for Learman and Jareau to sit and join Morgan and Reid.

"What about it, Detective?" Hotchner asked, sitting. "*Do* you think John Doe was murdered somewhere else?"

Learman let out a humorless chuckle. "Could have gone either way. No signs of struggle in the alley, but also a good deal of blood in the Dumpster. Not to mention that John Doe didn't have any defensive wounds . . . and was stoned out of his mind on Rohypnol."

Hotchner's only reply was a tiny shrug.

"What about you, Agent Hotchner?" Learman asked. "What does this do to the profile you're developing, which incidentally I would have thought you'd be sharing with us Lawrence cops along about now?"

"Just a minor setback," Hotchner said.

"Minor setback? You think looking for *two*

suspects and not *one* is just a minor setback? Even though it upsets every assumption you've made so far?"

"It's not going to interfere greatly," Hotchner said, "in developing the profile. In fact, it's helpful, because we're on the right track now."

"Goody for you," Learman said. He got up. "You people keep reading your tea leaves. I'm going to get back to what we in the real world call police work."

And the detective went quickly out, with Jareau giving her teammates a little "oh boy" smile as she trailed after the man with whom she must liaise.

The profilers sat and thought. For perhaps five minutes, no one said anything, and no one did anything, not anything overt.

They were thinking.

The team dynamic was something they had run across before — Jacksonville, Florida, last fall, for instance. The Jacksonville killers had been a husband-and-wife team — Amber and Tony Canardo. They had terrorized Jacksonville for three years before the BAU team took them down. Many such teams pursued their evil goals over the course of history, giving the BAU group plenty of experience to draw upon when developing their profile.

Suddenly Reid spoke, like one emerging from a trance.

"One aspect sometimes brought up with team killers is *folie à deux,*" he said, "a rare psychological condition in which one person copies and incorporates the delusions and psychotic patterns of another person into his own personality."

Morgan, rather than asking Reid where he'd come up with that mouthful, said, "I've read about that. According to convicted British team killer, Ian Brady, *folie à deux* could only occur 'if the target person is fertile soil in which such proposals can readily take root.' "

Reid, nodding, completed the quote: " 'In other words, the criminal desire must already be present.' Which certainly seemed to be the case when Kenneth Bianchi and Angelo Buono, the two men known by the singular moniker the Hillside Strangler, worked in a similar manner."

Hotchner, staring into nothing but his thoughts, said, "Buono managed the more pliable Bianchi, but both were involved in the murders of the prostitutes."

Reid said, "And of course another necessary element for a killing team is dominance and submission."

Morgan said, "Someone has to be in

charge."

"Two chiefs," Hotchner said, "with no Indians means a team cannot exist."

"Careful," Morgan said. "There's more than one kind of killing team. . . ."

With an enthusiastic lift of his eyebrows, Reid picked up: "The *In Cold Blood* killers, Dick Hickock and Perry Smith? They were driven by Hickock's fantasy of finding wealth in a safe in a farmhouse . . . right here in Kansas. They decided, early on, at Hickock's insistence, that no witnesses be left behind."

"And when there was no money," Morgan said, "they slaughtered the family, anyway."

Hotchner raised a gently lecturing forefinger. "Remember, more than one explanation for that was offered."

Reid, nodding, said, "Yes, but both came from the submissive Perry Smith — in one version, he claimed he and Dick each killed two of the Clutter family; then later, citing the fact that Dick's parents were still alive and his weren't? Perry claimed to have killed all *four* of the Clutters himself. In that team — at least for the most part — Hickock was the master, and Smith the weapon."

The room fell silent again as the profilers returned to their thoughts.

Hotchner was back where he'd been at

the start, right before the case had begun, thinking about the school killings that were happening too often this time of year.

The Columbine killers, Eric Harris and Dylan Klebold, fell somewhere between the *In Cold Blood* pair. Harris was the more vocal of the two, but Klebold seemed as deeply involved in the fantasy as his dominant partner.

They both planned on leaving behind a far greater legacy of death and destruction than they'd been able to wreak.

The Jacksonville couple, the Canardos, had been a husband-wife team, where the woman was dominant and her husband/accomplice submissive. Their psychosis was hers, with the husband along for the ride due to his devotion to his master, rather than out of any personal urge to kill.

Tony Canardo might, or might not, have killed on his own; but with the influence of the dominant partner, he had become a killing machine, Amber using sex to help keep her submissive in line.

And even in same-sex teams a sexual element was often in play. The submissive might be in love with the dominant, even though never acting on the impulse.

Hotchner met Reid's eyes, then Morgan's. He said simply, "Loeb and Leopold."

Both profilers began to nod. . . .

Eighteen-year-old Nathan Leopold was deeply in love with his dominant partner, nineteen-year-old Richard Loeb, when the two snatched fourteen-year-old Bobby Franks and killed him in Chicago in May of 1924. After the murder, the pair sent a ransom note to the Franks family in hopes of extorting money, even though they had already killed the boy. Jacob Franks, Bobby's father, was about to get into a Yellow cab to go pay the ransom when the police called to say young Bobby's body had been found.

Reid said, "It's not comforting, knowing that Leopold and Loeb sent *their* ransom note *after* killing their victim, if the homeless killing and the Bonder abduction *are* one case."

Hotchner said nothing and neither did Morgan.

Finally Morgan lifted a cautionary palm. "We may have wandered into a Loeb and Leopold of our own. But there's no evidence yet to support that."

Hotchner nodded. "We need to stay focused on what we do know." His cell phone chirped. He checked the caller ID, then pushed the button to accept the call. "Garcia — tell me you have something."

"I do," she said cheerily. "I've ID'd your John Doe. Reid gave me a name — Frank Webster. DOD matched his fingerprints from his service record. He was an honorable discharge. Seems like he was a good guy. Not so much as a traffic ticket until his wife died. Then, he slipped into a depression that he obviously never recovered from. Lost his house, ended up on the street, and finally wound up your killer's victim."

"Good job," Hotchner said, getting ready to sign off.

"Like they say in the infomercials," Garcia said, "but wait, there's more. . . ."

"Garcia, save the 'cute' for Morgan."

"Sorry." Her voice shifted into strictly business-like gear: "We received a video from IndieVU.com."

"Which is what?"

"A website that showcases short films, and previews of independent films. Works in progress, cinematic bits and pieces by amateurs and up-and-coming professionals."

Hotchner frowned, trying not to get irritated with this very valuable resource. "Why are we interested in that kind of website?"

"Are you near your laptop?" Garcia asked, answering his question with one of her own, something Hotchner hated, although he did it frequently himself.

"Yes."

"Well, take a look at the video I'm streaming to you. The webmaster e-mailed us this clip for the same reason sites send us sexual predator videos — they think it may be real."

"Is it?"

"I believe it is — brace yourself: it seems to show the murder of Frank Webster."

Hotchner, at his laptop, waved the others over to gather around. He tapped the touch pad and the video filled the screen.

They all watched silently as a man in a suit, Frank Webster, sat on a sofa in what looked like an otherwise bare room.

"What's this?" Reid asked.

"Video from Garcia," Hotchner said. "Frank Webster's murder, she says."

"What, re-created?"

"I don't think so."

They watched as another person entered the frame from the right — in black from head to toe, including a ski mask with only eyes and mouth openings.

The fear in the man's face — as the killer withdrew a long knife from somewhere — was nothing an actor could manufacture. But what truly struck the clinical Hotchner was the high quality of the recording.

This wasn't some lousy old video camcorder: the killers were using some sort of high-end digital camera.

They watched mutely as the killer closed in on the victim.

Webster tried to run, but something — the drugs or simple loss of balance — made him slip and fall. The killer waited for his prey to rise as far as his knees, then caught Webster in the shoulder with the first blow.

The older man shrieked (challenging the laptop's speakers) and went to the ground, rolled away and again tried to run in the enclosed space — was it a trashed-out mobile home?

Webster had nowhere to go, though, and the killer was on him after two steps, stabbing him twice in the back. The first blow was low, the kidney wound Dr. Ohka had told them about.

Then came the second, the higher blow, the killing blow. As Webster crumpled to the floor, the killer jerked on something on the wall and drapes fell away, whiting out the shot with the light of the bright day pouring through the uncovered windows.

That was where the tape ended.

Talking into the phone, Hotchner said, "Have you traced it?"

"Trying, Chief, but they routed it through way many different places before it showed up at IndieVU.com. I'm trying, but it's going to take time."

"Thanks, Garcia."

"There's one more thing, sir."

"What's that?"

"I've seen this action before."

"You *have?*"

"Not this exact scene per se, but the movie that it's modeled on, I have, yes, sir."

"This killing is . . . patterned on something from a movie?"

"Yes," Garcia said. "From an Italian horror film called *Il Morte Improvviso,* or *Sudden Death.* It's a late eighties flick made by Italian director Giuseppe Serna."

"And this is a replay of action from that film?"

"The tearing of the curtains, the white out, the stabbing, it's all pretty much a straight rip-off of Serna's scene."

"So you feel pretty sure our killers have seen this movie?"

"I am totally sure, sir. And I think I know who you're looking for — I don't mean names, I mean . . . the *type* of person."

"Well?"

Garcia seemed hesitant. Then: "My guess is you're after a couple of gorehounds."

"Couple of what?"

"Gorehounds. Film fans, predominantly young men, who watch these horror movies as a way of dealing with their inner rage."

"Or," Hotchner said, "as a way of inflaming it."

"Would seem so in this case. But a lot of normal people like those kind of movies. I mean, I've seen *Sudden Death.* It's a, uh, very cool movie, in its way. Sir."

"Do you think there are more of these videos out there?"

"I'm looking, all the usual places, starting with You Tube and Google Video on down to the most obscure sites. If they're there, I'll find them."

"Thanks, Garcia."

"Yes, sir."

He rang off and filled the other two in.

Morgan, his eyebrows up, said, "That Garcia's a better profiler than we are. Anybody notice anything about this homemade horror film?"

"Well," Reid said, "it may be the first proof that so-called 'snuff films' are more than an urban legend."

Morgan shook his head. "It's real, yes, we're witnessing Frank Webster's murder, but it's more than just *staged* to resemble some Italian horror flick."

"Not following you," Hotchner said.

"Hotch, it's *edited*. There are inserts of the killer on the move — of the knife in his hand. Action staged after or apart from the killing itself."

Hotchner looked at Morgan for a long time, asking a question silently that finally drew a nod from the other profiler. Reid also nodded.

Hotchner got back on his cell and told Learman, "We're ready to give your people our profile. Let's get them together."

The bullpen was crowded with a mix of detectives and uniformed officers, some in chairs, others leaning against the walls, several nursing cups of coffee, most with notepads and pens out. At the far end of the room, Hotchner, Reid, Morgan, and Jareau held court, Learman next to them.

"All right," Learman said. "Let's listen up. These are the folks from the FBI; you've seen them around here, last few days. They have a profile for us of our homeless killers, so pay attention."

"Killers?" one of the detectives asked.

"Yes," Hotchner said. "*Killers* — plural. We're dealing with a killing duo."

The officers around the room traded looks. They'd all been certain they were seeking a lone killer.

Somebody in back said, "Batman and Robin? You have to be kidding."

"Actually," Hotchner said, his voice a blade of authority that cut through the skeptical atmosphere, "we have quite a bit of information about team killers."

"Such as?" another asked.

We are in an alley. A homeless person searches through a Dumpster.

"These killers," Hotchner said, "are not confident enough to confront their victims . . . not without some sort of enticement, either food or money."

A hand in a dark sleeve comes out of the darkness and offers the homeless person a bill. The homeless person follows the dark-clothed figure down the alley and the two disappear.

Morgan said, "Once they have the victim under their wing, they take him or her somewhere, ostensibly to feed them."

They are in a restaurant now, the dark figure sitting with his back to us, the victim across the table, eating.

Morgan continued: "But while the victim is eating, they slip him or her Rohypnol in the food."

As the victim eats, the dark figure drops a pill into his drink.

Reid said, "Then they take the victim off

somewhere private. From the video we just saw, which we will share with you, it may be an abandoned mobile home. Which would seem to be the crime scene for the Webster murder, the victim found in the Dumpster."

The killers lead the victim inside a mobile home where they force him to bathe and shave, then they lay out a thrift-store suit.

"They clean him up," Morgan said, "dress him in the costume of their choice, and kill him by acting out scenes from little-seen, violent horror movies that have taken on a deep significance for them."

As one killer films the murder, the other commits it, images of Italian horror movies flashing across the walls of the trailer as Frank Webster succumbs and is murdered. The attacker pulls down the drapes and the picture whites out.

"One will be dominant," Hotchner said. "He will generally be the smarter of the two, but not always. It's the dominant's fantasy of hatred and violence, however, that they're playing out."

"They'll be young," Reid said. "Probably no more than twenty-five at most. They have little experience in killing. They're still learning their craft, although they are becoming increasingly confident with each murder."

"They don't want to be caught," Morgan said.

"Doesn't that go without saying?" a detective asked.

Morgan shook his head. "Not always. Sometimes a killer will know what he's doing is wrong but be unable to stop himself. He *needs* us to stop him. Those people usually put up very little fight when captured. They're actually relieved, on some level. *These* guys?" He shook his head again. "These guys have an agenda and they're nowhere near the end of it. They will probably not go easy. They should be considered armed and dangerous."

"What is their plan?" a uniformed cop asked.

"There's no way to know for sure," Hotchner said.

"Some profile," the cop muttered.

Hotchner rose to his full height and his eyes fell on the cop with laser-beam intensity. "What do you know about Columbine?"

"Uh . . ."

"Wasn't that far from here," Hotchner said. "Eric Harris and Dylan Klebold, what do you know about them and their crimes?"

"Thirteen dead," the cop said, and swallowed. "Twenty-five wounded."

"And a wall blown out of the library," Morgan added.

"One of thirty bombs planted around the school," Reid said.

"The largest," Morgan said, "was made out of a pipe bomb, two propane tanks and other fuel cylinders. It was in the kitchen. Right next to the cafeteria where many students were hiding. If they had been successful in setting that off, hundreds more could have died."

Hotchner said, "They planned their attack to begin at eleven a.m., because that's when the most students would be in the cafeteria. From there, according to Harris's journal, they intended to carry the massacre to the neighboring houses, then hijack a plane and crash it into New York City."

"No way," the cop said.

"Way," Morgan said. "It's all there. That was their plan — they just didn't get to carry it all out."

Hotchner said, "That's why we can't tell you the plan of the killers here in Lawrence . . . but for now, let's assume they intend to keep killing until we catch them."

"Oh," Reid said, as an afterthought, "and the Columbine killers? They made homemade movies of violent fantasy, as well. If that's helpful, at all."

Suddenly none of the cops seemed to be taking the BAU profilers — and their profile — anything but dead serious.

Chapter Seven

Supervisory Special Agent Jason Gideon wasn't as young as he used to be. But he didn't mind, because he knew more now.

Exercise kept him in good shape for this hard job, though his days of running the confidence course were behind him — a knee went balky, whenever the weather turned cold, or if he ran too much. Otherwise, his body had held up well despite nearly thirty years of wear and tear working for the Bureau.

He rolled over in the uncomfortable motel-room bed, turned off the alarm, and while still on the mattress did a series of stretching exercises, hearing bones pop like little muffled gunshots. Traveling this much made him feel like Goldilocks: this bed was too soft, that bed too hard, this mattress too lumpy, that one about as thick as a paper towel . . . and the only one that felt just right was half a country away in D.C.

Then he slipped off the bed and dropped to the floor for a quick fifty push-ups and twenty-five sit-ups.

Lousy beds in motels from coast to coast were just one of the perks that never made the Bureau recruitment brochures, along with jet lag, miserable fast food, and stale police department coffee. Nonetheless, this was a job he loved beyond reason — though he'd once warned Reid, "It will gnaw at your soul."

Even as he showered, he was already back at work, his mind as slippery as the soap as he moved in and around the different facts and facets of the case, viewing them from new angles, seeking new intersections.

Fifteen minutes later Gideon was getting into jeans and white shirt with maroon pinstripes (he had never been the button-down Brooks Brothers kind of agent that Hotch, God love him, so perfectly embodied). As he slipped on his black loafers, he mulled the missing student they were searching for.

Then, over a light breakfast in the motel lobby (a decent fruit plate, for a change), his mind wrestled with possibilities inherent in any disappearance, even as he glanced over the morning's *USA Today*.

When Emily Prentiss came down to join

him, somberly chic in a black blouse and matching slacks, they exchanged pleasantries; but as she nibbled her half-a-bagel breakfast, they already were both hard at work.

Prentiss finished her coffee just as Gideon completed the crossword puzzle in *USA Today.* Doing this weekday mornings kept his brain as toned as daily calisthenics did his body. And puzzle-solving was helpful, even if the psychology of a criminal was seldom as easy as five across and ten down.

Anyway, these little activities provided Gideon with a routine in a job that put him on the road more often than a country-western musician. Each of his BAU teammates had his or her own tricks for dealing with the boredom and vicissitudes of life on the road: Reid and Morgan had their iPods, while Prentiss, Jareau, and Hotchner read books and magazines, fiction and nonfiction both.

And, of course, once a day, Hotchner checked in with his wife to see how she and their young son, Jack, were doing. Gideon envied, but certainly did not begrudge, his friend for what appeared an idyllic home life; and he knew Hotch's obsessive dedication to the job was in part an extension of protecting his own family by removing monsters from society.

"You want another cup?" Prentiss asked.

He smiled and shook his head. "No, thanks. Any more caffeine and I'll have the heart rate of a rabbit."

"And that's a bad thing?" She got up and strolled over to the coffee urn.

As he watched her pour herself another, Gideon was struck by something an imprisoned serial killer had once said to him: "We're the same, you and me — that's how you caught me. We're brothers under the flesh." This chilling statement had lingered with Gideon because it contained a kernel of truth.

The prototypical serial killer was a quiet loner, much like everyone on the BAU team. Of the five profilers (as well as non-profiler Jareau), only Hotch had a wife and child.

Then again, Gideon didn't know every single thing about his teammates, nor they about him. Co-workers who spent this much time together tended to carefully guard the nooks and crannies of their private lives; and when the co-workers were *profilers,* well . . .

When Prentiss sat back down, Gideon asked, "Are you seeing anyone right now?"

The question caught her off guard, and

she took a quick sip of her coffee to cover. "No. Not for a while, actually. It's the job, I guess. We're on the road *so* much. . . ."

He nodded. "Didn't mean to intrude. Your other posts didn't require this much travel, I take it."

"No. This is all new."

"It does take its toll."

Gideon knew too well how hard it was to maintain a relationship outside of this work. He didn't pursue the conversation any further: he sensed Emily's discomfort and, anyway, there was the job.

He snapped his cell phone off his belt and found a business card in his wallet, then punched in Special Agent Morris Parker's number.

On the second ring: "Parker."

"Gideon. Good morning."

"Quiet night. No calls."

This, of course, was no surprise: had the kidnapper called, Parker would have got hold of Gideon, no matter what time.

Gideon asked, "How's the family holding up?"

A pause.

Gideon figured the Bonders were in the room with Parker, who would be moving out of earshot.

Finally, Gideon heard a door shut, and

Parker said, "They stayed locked in their bedroom all night. Judging from the look of them, I doubt they slept much. Ever see footage of the survivors of Auschwitz when the G.I.s pulled them out? Their expressions?"

"Yes. Haunted."

"That's it. This is my third kidnap case in fifteen years, and if I retire before the next one, it's still too soon."

"Detective Warren's picking us up in about five minutes," Gideon said, cutting off Parker's existential bellyaching. "Then we're going to the university to see what we can gather."

"Makes sense."

"You guys okay over there?"

"Minet's making a breakfast run. We'll survive without you."

"Agent Jareau handy?"

"I'll get her."

Jareau got on the line and said, "Good morning. Wish there were better news."

"Morning. You may want to consider heading back to the law enforcement center, if you feel the Bonders can get along without you."

"You'd rather have me on hand at the station, where I can deal with media from either case?"

"Exactly."

"I'll check in with the Bonders, then hook up with Detective Learman."

"Good."

Promptly at eight, Detective Warren strode into the lobby, her dark hair down today, bouncing softly on the shoulders of a navy blue pullover. The belt of her gray slacks held her holstered weapon and from a chain around her neck dangled her gold shield.

Very attractive woman, Gideon thought. *And smart, smarter than Detective Learman, of course, but even smarter than that.*

Warren and Prentiss exchanged good mornings, then the detective smiled at Gideon. "Sleep well?"

Gideon smiled back, not dignifying the lumpy bed upstairs with a comment. "I'll sleep better when Kathy Bonder is safely home."

Warren wagged her head toward the street. "Well, I have a warrant in the car. That's a start."

"Yes it is. Found a judge first thing this morning?" He grinned at her. "You *are* a detective."

"I try. His Honor didn't quite know why you thought we'd need it, and frankly neither do I — a missing KU student? They'll *want* to help find her."

Gideon shrugged. "Anyone with the university should, but remember, there's a lot of red tape protecting the privacy of students these days."

Prentiss said, "And any friends of Kathy's we talk to may have their own reasons for not wanting their rooms poked around in — cops and FBI running across a stash of hash, for example, might not appeal."

"Anyway," Gideon said, "we don't want to waste time waiting for a warrant if we *do* need it."

Warren seemed on the verge of pointing out the time *she'd* have wasted, should they not need it; but instead she merely nodded and showed the profilers to her car.

Twenty minutes later, they were parked and walking across the wide green campus to the registrar's office. This beautiful day was already heading toward today's anticipated high in the mid-eighties. Students, humpbacked with bookbags, walked to and from class, wrapped up in their own lives, their own thoughts, paying scant attention to the man and two women moving through — new teachers, they probably thought, if they thought anything at all.

The building was three-story brick with four sets of double doors. The registrar's office, on the first floor, was the last door on the right. As they entered, a self-important-looking little woman in a blue blouse and black slacks rose from behind a metal desk and positioned herself at the wood counter bisecting the room. Her black hair drawn back in a severe bun, her spadelike face pinched, she nonetheless greeted Detective Warren and the BAU agents with a thin smile.

"May I help you?" she asked.

Badge proffered, Warren introduced herself and the profilers, concluding, "We need to ask about one of your students."

"I see." The woman's smile had long since faded. "Which student?"

"Kathy Bonder," the detective said. "We'd need a list of her classes, and any other information you may have on file."

"I'm sorry." Her spine stiffened with bureaucratic resolve. "I'm sure you have a perfectly good reason. But we're not allowed to hand out personal information about our students."

Gideon stepped forward. "Excuse me. We gave you our names, but I didn't catch yours."

"It's Mrs. Pankly."

Not a good sign, Gideon thought, *this gate-keeper referring to herself so formally.*

He gave her a sad smile. "Mrs. Pankly,

Kathy has gone missing."

The woman touched her lower lip, and the humanity behind her eyes shone out momentarily. "How terrible. Unfortunately, that doesn't —"

Prentiss said, "She's been kidnapped."

"I wish I could help," the woman said, her genuine concern unable to break through her officious catch-22 dedication.

Warren looked at Gideon, as if to say, *You were right,* and the detective withdrew the warrant from her purse and handed it to Mrs. Pankly, who scanned it quickly, then surrendered with another thin smile.

"I'll attend to this immediately," she said, letting them know she wasn't only proper but efficient.

Back in just over two minutes with a small stack of paper in a manila file folder, the woman handed it to Warren, who said, "Thank you for your cooperation."

Mrs. Pankly seemed not to notice the trace of sarcasm in the detective's tone, merely saying, "Glad to be able to help."

A few minutes later, the trio was sharing a table in the student union, going over Kathy Bonder's file. Around them, students were grabbing a late breakfast, studying at tables alone or in quiet groups, reading the campus paper and sipping designer coffees, or just passing through on their way to their next class.

At their table, Warren, Prentiss, and Gideon each divied up the sheets.

"Good grades," Prentiss said. "Straight A's."

Warren said, "Bills paid up. Not so much as an overdue library book."

Gideon perused Kathy Bonder's current schedule. "Taking fifteen hours. Film course, drama class, a writing class, psych 101 and Trig."

"Trig's pretty heavy-duty math," Warren noted, "for somebody who wants to act for a living."

"A small anomaly like that," Gideon said, "is exactly why we should talk to her teachers." He began to rub his hands together. "The more we know about Kathy, the more we might be able to learn about her patterns. The kidnapper took her off campus without raising suspicion — how? Why Kathy? These are questions we may come closer to answering, once we know more about the victim and her routine."

Prentiss, nodding, said, "What about her best friend?"

From a slacks pocket, Warren withdrew a notebook and flipped it open to fan forward a few pages to a name the Bonders had provided last night. "Abby Querin," she said.

Kathy's best friend since junior high. The two had entered KU at the same time, both interested in film and drama.

Though Gideon had only seen for a moment the photo that the Bonders provided the police, it — like the victim photos in his office — was etched in his mind. Young Dr. Reid could remember damn near anything; but Gideon only had a photographic memory for tragedy.

Gideon asked, "Was Kathy's friend Abby the slim brunette in the photo Mrs. Bonder gave you for ID purposes?"

"Why yes," Warren said. "She was. . . ."

In his mind's eye Gideon could see Abby, a brunette as slender as blonde Kathy, hair flowing down over her shoulders, warm gray eyes, a fetchingly crooked smile. Jeans and a gold, ruffle-trimmed, scoop-necked tee.

"I'll track down Querin," Warren was saying, "if you two want to interview Kathy's professors."

"Fine," Gideon said. "Meet back here in two hours?"

Warren nodded. "That enough time to interview five professors?"

Gideon shrugged and smiled. "We'll give it the college try."

Professors could, of course, be windy; but the brutal truth was, on a campus this size, few of the profs would know much more about Kathy than her name, if that. And forty-five minutes and four professors later, the two profilers had learned little more than they'd had going in; and Gideon was wondering how they were going to spend the next hour and a quarter.

To give them their due, the professors had known much more about Kathy than just her name, their opinion a shared one: bright girl, attractive, vivacious, attentive, did good work, got it in on time, never caused trouble or had problems. Those particular attributes, however, probably put her in the same category as about ninety percent of the other female students in those classes.

Gideon was getting exasperated as they moved toward the building that housed Kathy's last class. They were within sight of the two-story brick structure when Gideon's cell phone vibrated on his belt. He stopped to answer it.

"Me," Hotchner announced.

For the next five minutes the two federal agents traded information about their respective cases.

"You've made progress," Gideon told Hotchner.

"Yes. But nothing seems to tie in to your kidnapping."

"That's not a bad thing. We should connect again in . . . four hours?"

"Four hours."

As he replaced his cell phone on his belt, Gideon glanced at Prentiss, who had only heard his side of the conversation.

He watched her, "Do you know what a 'gorehound' is?"

She gave him a quizzical look. "Someone who watches too many horror movies."

Gideon half-smiled. "Hotch *said* you'd know."

"Is that a compliment? *You* don't know that term?"

He shrugged and favored her with a wan smile. "Can't keep up with everything. I knew there were enthusiasts for those kind of films — I didn't know they had a name."

"Then I take it you're not a subscriber to *Fangoria* magazine."

"No. Are you?"

"Gideon," she said, with a wicked smile, "some things remain on a 'need to know' basis."

He filled her in on the rest of what he had learned.

"Odd," he said.

"Yeah, it is." She frowned. "What is?"

"Here we're checking out a film class, and the homeless-victim killers are filming their crimes. Film buffs filming murders . . ."

She was still frowning. "That *is* odd, as in odd coincidence, if it is a coincidence."

"I wonder."

Gideon made a mental note as they entered the building. The class room was on the second floor about halfway down on the right. Although the lights were out, class was in session. Peering through a narrow window in the door, the two agents realized a movie was playing on a screen above the lecture podium.

Gideon couldn't quite see the screen, nor hear the movie, because the sound was turned down and the professor was speaking from somewhere toward the back of the room, lecturing over the movie — a real-time DVD commentary.

Through the door, Gideon heard the professor say, "They were made seven years apart, with incredible similarities: same story, same star, same drunken best friend, same young heartthrob to help them, the same wizened mentor figure, even the same director . . . but still both found an audience, and were big box-office, managing to mine different material in the same source."

Prentiss whispered, "Okay, I give — what

movies is he talking about?"

Gideon said, "*Rio Bravo* and *El Dorado*. John Wayne, directed by Howard Hawks — 1959 and 1967 respectively."

"And you didn't know *'gorehound'?*"

The projector stopped, the lights came on, and the professor said, "That's it for today, film fans — but between flicks, read Gehring's *World of Comedy* before I see you again."

A collective groan went up from the class — a sound that hadn't changed in all the years since Gideon himself had sat in college classes, unfortunately *not* getting credit for watching classic westerns.

Gideon had to take a quick step back as the door swung open and fifteen or so students spilled out into the hallway. Other doors in the corridor opened as well, the population swelling dramatically. Gideon and Prentiss waited for the tide to subside and ducked into the classroom. The professor — carrying a notebook and several DVD cases — was moving from the rear to a desk at front left.

The professor was Gideon's height and about the same age, thinner, with straight, unreceding black hair coming in white at the sideburns. He wore a well-groomed black mustache and his gray eyes were sharply inquisitive.

"I'm afraid you missed the feature," he said jovially. "May I help you?"

Gideon asked, "Professor Roger Caine?"

"Afraid you have me at a disadvantage," Caine said, setting his materials on his desk, as the agents approached.

"Special Agents Gideon and Prentiss," Gideon said, showing his FBI ID. "We're here to talk about —"

"Kathy Bonder," Caine said glumly.

Prentiss and Gideon exchanged surprised glances.

"News travels fast on a college campus," Caine said. "Bad news, even more so. Cell calls, text messages, the brave new world."

Gideon asked, "What have you heard, Professor?"

Caine shrugged. "The rumor is she's disappeared. The wild rumor is she's been kidnapped. All I know for certain is that Miss Bonder was in class on Monday."

"Not yesterday?"

"We're a Monday, Wednesday, Friday class. Didn't meet yesterday."

Prentiss asked, "What can you tell us about Kathy?"

Again Caine shrugged. "Probably what her other teachers have said — smart young woman. She participates in class, always shows up prepared. Never has had, or created, any problems in this class."

Gideon said, "Anything else you could share would be appreciated, Professor."

He considered that. "Well, I would say she's a talented actress. She could actually make it in Hollywood, if things go her way, and she can shake some of the bad habits actors pick up doing stage plays in school."

Prentiss said, "That leads us to a question we asked her parents — could she be enough of an actress to stage her own kidnapping?"

A little smile played at the corner of Caine's mouth. "To what end? . . . I mean, she is, probably, good enough to pull a stunt like that and get away with it; but she wouldn't! I know her family, and spent time with her — I'm one of her advisors, and I can assure you she's a levelheaded young woman." He shook his head with some feeling. "Just not the sort of thing she would do."

Gideon asked, "How much time have you spent with Miss Bonder?"

The professor bristled, but Gideon's expression and tone had been mild, and after Caine studied Gideon a few seconds, he backed down as he said, "Kathy started getting into stage productions as soon as she arrived on campus, as a freshman. She also got into the film production end right away."

"As an actress?"

"As an actress, in other students' film projects. But she's also a filmmaker herself — everyone in the program has to be. And I must say, she's been a real asset to both the film and drama departments."

Other students were starting to file in and sit down now.

Caine's goodwill seemed about as used up as the time between his lectures. "Is that everything I can do for you?"

"Just one more question," Gideon said.

"Make it a quick one."

"Are any of your students the kind of film buff who might be considered a gore-hound?"

Caine let out a short laugh. "Practically all of them. Tarantino is God to them. I talk *Vertigo* or *Night of the Hunter,* and they talk *Saw* or *Hostel.*"

"How about students particularly interested in Italian horror films?"

"Lot of these kids are hip to Mario and Lamberto Bava and Dario Argento and so on."

Shaking his head, Gideon said, "This student . . . or maybe two students, collaborators possibly . . . would be different."

"Different how?"

"Not very confident around people."

Caine shrugged. "Again, that's nearly all of them. They're college students — they don't know anything about the real world. They're naturally lacking in confidence, many of them. Kids interested in the arts aren't necessarily outgoing."

"They're seeking shelter in their talent and their enthusiasms," Gideon said. "Yes. But this one never talks in class, never volunteers. He would have trouble looking you in the eye during a conversation. He would be prone to fits of rage when things didn't go his way."

The professor stared at Gideon. Then: "That sounds like Beck."

"Beck?"

"Yes. Becker Chapin."

Prentiss asked, "Student of yours?"

"Not current. Former. Last semester."

Gideon asked, "What kind of student?"

"A hard worker certainly, and he wrote decent critical papers; but his filmmaking was frankly terrible, and he couldn't take criticism. When I gave him an 'F' on his final last year, he blew like a geyser . . . screamed, yelled, ranted, then stormed out."

"And after that?"

"After that I never saw him again." Concern grooved Caine's forehead. "Do you think Beck could have something to do with Kathy's disappearance?"

Gideon's answer was a question of his own: "Did they know each other?"

Caine shrugged. "I don't know for sure. I don't think they were in the same classes, and I'm sure we can check that easily enough . . . but they were certainly in the same field of study. I wouldn't be the least bit surprised if they'd crossed paths."

Prentiss asked, "Any idea where we can find Becker Chapin?"

"I'm sorry, no. The registrar's office could probably help you, though — I don't even know if he's still a student here. Haven't seen him since the blowup, last November."

Gideon did not want to go back to the registrar's gatekeeper, but that trip seemed inevitable now. "What else can you tell us about him?"

Caine seemed puzzled. "Nothing, I don't think. What did you have in mind?"

"Well, for instance, did he have any good friends in class?"

"No, not that I remember."

"Did he come and go with the same person, or group of people every day?"

"No, he was more of a loner. He was a

crude filmmaker, who lacked the patience and, frankly, talent to improve; and when I told him as much, he . . . well, I didn't think anything of it at the time . . . he threatened to kill me."

"To kill you?"

"After I failed him on his final project. He was so enthusiastic about it, he turned it in early, before Thanksgiving; and it was painful to have to disappoint a kid like that, who'd worked so hard."

"What sort of film did Beck make?"

"A derivative horror film with laughable ketchup-bottle special effects, and unbelievably awful over-the-top acting, and scenes ripped off from several low budget slasher movies. More than one from Italy — I remember in particular a clumsy re-do of a scene from *Suspiria*."

Around them, the students — all in their seats by now — shifted nervously, trying to listen, and seem like they weren't.

Gideon said, "Professor Caine, a student threatened to kill you. Did you report it to the administration?"

"Certainly not. It was just an emotional outburst. You know, the way someone says, 'I could just kill that guy.' "

In these days of Columbine and Virginia Tech, the professor's attitude was in itself dangerous; but Gideon wasn't here to be guest lecturer.

Quietly Caine asked, "You think Beck kidnapped Kathy?"

"Too early to say. But we'll find out. Do you believe in the *auteur* theory, Professor?"

"The director as author of the film? I do, actually."

"So do I. We deal with *auteurs* of murder, Professor Caine, and like all filmmakers, each has a distinctive signature."

Gideon and Prentiss thanked the professor for his time, then started back toward the student union.

As they walked, Gideon asked, "What's your gut tell you about Becker Chapin?"

"My gut?" Prentiss asked. "Haven't I heard you say profiling is built on logic and probability?"

Smiling, Gideon said, "It is. But don't discount gut instinct; some inner part of you is processing logic and probability and adding in common sense and all of your earthly experience. May not be perfect, but the longer you do this, the more your gut instincts tell you."

"Well," she said, going back to Gideon's question and dodging it a little, "Chapin fits the profile. He lacks confidence, he's within the age parameters, and he is, by at least one witness's testimony, a gorehound fascinated with Italian horror movies. If he failed around Thanksgiving, that might be the stressor that sent him into a homicidal rage. The murders started right around then."

"Yes, but what about your gut?"

Her eyes widened. "When Professor Caine started nodding every time you mentioned another trait? The hair on the back of my neck stood up. I think Chapin's our guy."

"Me too," Gideon said softly. "But the question that keeps nagging me is, if the killers and the kidnappers are the same people, why have they been killing homeless people, only now to kidnap upper-middle-class Kathy Bonder?"

"Escalation?"

"Yes, absolutely, but why *her?* Plenty of girls in the film and drama departments around here — why Kathy Bonder? If I knew that, we would know if Chapin is one of the homeless-killing UnSubs."

They were halfway back to the union when Gideon phoned Garcia.

"Yes, sir," Garcia said when she picked up, obviously having checked to see his number on her caller ID.

"Garcia, I need background on Becker

Chapin. He is, or was, a KU student."

"I'll get right on it, sir."

As was usual when she spoke to him, Garcia's voice had an eager puppy quality. She always wanted to please the members of the team, but with Gideon, this went even further. Somehow, in him, she seemed to have found a paternal figure she needed desperately to please.

This quality both flattered and disturbed Gideon. A great deal of responsibility came with a relationship like this, and he always went out of his way to praise Garcia. But she was incredibly bright, meaning the praise had to be earned or it would sound wooden and artificial, and lose its significance.

So he just gave her a pleasant, crisp, "Thanks," but before she could hang up, added, "You figured out about the killing being on the internet, didn't you? Centered on the gorehounds?"

An embarrassed silence followed at the other end. Finally, she said, "Yes, sir."

"That was a good catch, Garcia — nice work."

"Thank you, sir. By the way, JJ sent me all the material connected to the Bonder kidnapping. I was studying a photo of Kathy Bonder that her mother sent?"

"I've seen it."

"I may have noticed something else significant. Kathy Bonder is the spitting image of an Italian actress — Lena Mercurtio. Not very well-known over here, but something of a star in Europe, in fact *the* star of *Il Morte Improvviso,* or *Sudden Death,* the movie the killers copied when they killed Frank Webster. Or am I just reading in?"

Gideon felt something cold coil in his stomach, a slumbering snake about to wake. "You may have 'just read in' the reason she was abducted. That's good work, Garcia. *Really* good."

When Gideon and Prentiss arrived back at the union, they were still a good forty-five minutes early to meet Warren. To their surprise, she was sitting at a table with an attractive young brunette Gideon immediately recognized as Abby Querin.

Except for the fact that today the young woman wore a blue KU T-shirt and denim skirt, Abby looked exactly as she had in the photo Gideon had glimpsed of Kathy Bonder and her longtime best friend.

As the two FBI agents approached the table, Gideon noticed Detective Warren was wearing her black, hexagonal-shaped glasses during the interview — she was farsighted, he realized, and wore them for close-up work, taking notes and scouring crime scenes.

Gideon and Prentiss took turns shaking hands with Abby Querin, who seemed to be holding up all right, though a tissue she clutched in her left hand and her red-rimmed eyes announced her concern for her missing friend.

"Do you need anything?" Gideon asked. "Coffee, water?"

Warren was sitting across from Abby, who shook her head, so Prentiss and Gideon took chairs to the young woman's left and right at the small, round table.

Warren removed her glasses, took a deep breath and let it out slowly. She looked weary, reminding Gideon that she and Leary had been working this case a lot longer than the BAU unit had.

"Abby was telling me," Warren said, "about what she and Kathy had planned to do after the school year ends."

"Really," Gideon said, giving Abby a reassuring smile. "Which was what?"

Dabbing at her eyes, Abby smiled. "We were going to work on a movie set. Kathy already had a part, and she talked to the director for me — she said he had a part for me, too. God, I'd've been thrilled just to be on set. I'd even be a grip . . . that's like, you know, a stagehand."

The girl looked to Gideon for confirmation that he understood.

He nodded that he knew and smiled. But, internally, alarms clanged within him. Something clicked, and he sat up straighter, a hunter with the scent of game in the air.

"I said I could do makeup," she added, oblivious to his posture. "Or hairstyling, anything — like I said, just to be on set. But an acting part!"

Gideon asked, "Would it happen to be a horror movie?"

Her smile widened, her enthusiasm for film momentarily overtaking her concern for her friend. "You've *heard* about the project?"

"In a manner of speaking." Gideon kept his tone conversational. "Do you know a young man named Becker Chapin? Used to be a student here?"

"Well, that's funny you should say that."

"Why?"

"He's the director!"

No knowing glance was exchanged by Gideon and Prentiss, but a mutual electricity ran through them.

Gideon had to proceed carefully here. "How did you meet him, Abby?"

She shook her head. "I never really did.

We were both students here, and he knew Kathy a little, so we would, like, nod at each other around campus and stuff. I don't think he really 'knew' me, except that I was a friend of Kathy's." She made air quotation marks as she said the word "knew."

Gideon nodded, keeping it casual. "How did you hear about the movie? Was it posted on a bulletin board, or online, or . . . ?"

"Oh, Kathy clued me in."

"Have you talked to Becker? In person or even on the phone? Or online, maybe?"

"No — just Kathy."

"What do you know about Becker?"

"Not a lot, really. Just that he was a student here, but he dropped out to concentrate on writing and filmmaking. He and his partner have been developing a script since last year some time."

Prentiss smiled and asked, "Who's his partner, do you know?"

"Dave . . . something. I never knew his last name."

"Oh?"

"Never met Dave," she said. "I don't think he ever took classes here. And, like I said, I only saw Beck around campus now and then, when he went here."

"When was the last time you saw him?"

Abby shrugged. "I dunno. Around

Thanksgiving, I suppose. Why?"

"Just covering the bases," Gideon said. "We'll want to talk to anyone who might have an idea of where Kathy is."

She nodded eagerly. "I understand. I'll do whatever I can, to pitch in. I'm sorry I can't be more helpful, but I haven't seen Becker in ages. Is he important in this?"

Gideon ignored that and asked, "You're sure you don't know anything about 'Dave,' his partner?"

"I'm sure I'm sure," Abby said. "Actually, I've only spoken to *Becker*, like . . . once. Kathy was the one who told me there even was a Dave, otherwise I wouldn't know anything about him."

Gideon gave her a perfunctory nod. Then lightly he asked, "Say, did Kathy know Becker well enough to grab a ride home with him? You know, or go off campus on an errand for some movie prop or whatever?"

"I don't know why not." She shrugged rather grandly. "Kath was up to be the lead in his movie, after all."

The pieces fell into place, all at once.

Gideon knew why the killers were recording their kills. Not as a souvenir of their deed, at least not entirely.

He turned to Prentiss and quietly said,

235

"They're making a movie."

"Of course they are."

"No, Emily — they are *making* a *movie.*"

And she got it, eyes wide. "Oh, hell," she said.

Warren frowned in confusion. "Did I come in late or something?"

Gideon returned his attention to Abby, gave her his warmest smile. "Thank you so much for your help. We have to go, now."

"Okay. Let me know if there's anything else! She's been my best friend forever."

"We know," Gideon said. "And we'll do everything we can to get you two back together."

"You think you can do that?"

"I do."

They were on the move, heading across the vast student-union cafeteria, threading through tables, Warren working to keep pace with the two FBI profilers.

"I'll call Garcia," Prentiss was saying.

"I'll call Hotch," Gideon was saying over her.

Warren still hadn't quite grasped what was happening. "What's going on, guys? Cut a girl a break."

As he jerked his phone off his belt, he told her, "Get the car. Becker Chapin is half the killing team. The reason they're cleaning up the homeless people?"

"Yes?"

"They're using them as bit players in their horror movie. But instead of the 'terrible' special effects Becker's professor complained about? The filmmakers are *really* murdering their actors."

"Christ," Warren said, her hand going to her mouth.

"And I'm pretty sure they're behind the kidnapping of Kathy Bonder, too," Gideon added. "Abby said it: 'She's up for the lead in their movie.' "

The chirping of Gideon's cell phone froze them.

"This is Gideon."

Jareau said, "Kathy Bonder's cell phone just got turned on."

Something in her voice didn't sit well with Gideon. "Where is it?"

"If Garcia is correct in her tracking of the GPS in your phone? Within a hundred feet of you."

Gideon's head whipped around as he scoured the nearby tables. He told Prentiss and Warren: "The phone's within one hundred feet."

They were surrounded by students, about half of whom were on their cell phones.

"Call the number," Gideon said.

"Can do," Jareau said and, within seconds, they heard a phone playing a song Gideon didn't recognize.

"That's 'Glamorous!' " Abby squealed from her table. "*Fergie!* It's Kathy's phone!"

Prentiss was first to it, students around them starting to look unnerved by the crazy people jumping about in their midst.

"It's all right, FBI!" Gideon said as he moved to the table where the no-longer-ringing pink phone sat atop a folded piece of paper, not twenty-five feet from where they'd sat with Abby.

"Ransom instructions?" Prentiss asked, referring to the note.

"We'll know soon enough," Gideon said.

Jareau called Gideon back. "Her voice mail kicked in."

"That's fine," Gideon said, and brought her up to speed, and clicked off.

Warren was already on her phone to the crime scene team.

"What we do know," Gideon said, "is that he was here."

"Which means," Prentiss said, "he knows *we're* here, too."

Snapping her phone shut, Warren said, "We need to lock down the building."

Although nodding his agreement, Gideon had little hope that that would do any good.

He could feel it.
The director of the tragedy was gone.

Chapter Eight

Just as Supervisory Special Agent Spencer Reid stepped out of the restroom, all hell broke loose.

Cell phones trilled, people hustled between desks and bulletin boards, others shouted to be heard over the cacophony. He had stepped away just long enough to answer nature's call, splash a little water on his face and wash his hands. Obviously, something had changed drastically in the last five minutes and he had the absurd thought that if he just closed the restroom door again, everything would be all right.

Hotchner came by, slipping on his suit coat and tucking his cell phone into a pocket. "Saddle up, Reid."

"Arrest in the offing, or another victim?"

"Unfortunately, the latter. Body discovered in the woods just north of town."

Reid grabbed his oversized bag off the desk and fell in behind Hotchner, Morgan, and Detective Learman, as they raced out of the Law Enforcement Center for their vehicles. Morgan got behind the wheel of the SUV with Hotch riding shotgun and Reid in the back. Learman climbed into his unmarked Crown Vic and led the way.

They wove through downtown traffic, emergency lights flashing, sirens blaring, rushing toward this latest crime scene. Strapped into the seat behind Morgan, Reid did his best to ignore how close they were coming to the cars around them.

As a human being, Reid dreaded what lay ahead; but as a psychologist, he viewed a fresh crime scene — the profilers normally arrived relatively late in the game — as an opportunity for new information, new insights, into an UnSub . . . in this case Un-Subs.

His cell phone rang. He snapped it off his belt and checked caller ID: *Prentiss.* Of any name on the BAU team, this one earned the slowest response time from him. Prentiss and he had not hit it off when she joined the team; he found her pushy and her sense of humor jarred. And things had not gotten better between them when he went through his rough patch earlier in the year.

True, he was at least as much at fault for their rocky relationship as she was: he had snapped at Prentiss more than once, and knew down deep he probably owed her an apology. Somehow he couldn't bring himself to do it. Maybe, like Hotch, he felt she'd been foisted on them by the higher-ups, with political agendas, and had not really earned her way onto the team.

Yet he knew her very outsider status should have brought them together. He, too — as the "boy" genius drafted by Gideon — had been subjected to similar prejudices when he'd joined the BAU team four years ago. Perhaps the problem was as simple as this: Prentiss was not Elle Greenaway, the member whose position Prentiss took.

But Prentiss had nothing to do with Elle's leaving; that was already history when she was assigned. Perhaps, Reid thought, his negative feelings reflected his own guilt for not doing more to help Elle, to support her and encourage Hotch to keep her on.

Maybe Prentiss was paying a price for the anger Reid felt at his own inaction.

All of this flashed through his mind in the second or two he took before answering her: "Reid."

"Where is everybody?" Prentiss asked.

She sounded shrill to him, but maybe he was reading too much into it. After all, Morgan and Hotchner had probably set their phones to vibrate after the call came in for the new victim. He would have, too, if they hadn't left in such a rush.

"There's been another murder," he said, working hard not to sound dismissive.

"Where?"

He filled her in, then she did the same with the kidnapping, including the possibility, even the probability, the team's two cases were intertwined. When they'd both clicked off, Reid passed Prentiss' update along to Hotch and Morgan.

"A note?" Hotchner asked. "Did it have instructions for delivering the ransom?"

"No one's read it yet. The crime scene analysts are moving very slowly. They want to make sure the paper's not booby-trapped, and of course they don't want to miss any possible evidence."

They all knew that some UnSubs booby-trapped various items to protect themselves. Some child pornographers, for example, kept vials of acid or small explosive charges attached to their hard drives, to destroy the evidence if a certain series of keystrokes was struck.

"So," Morgan asked, "who exactly is this Becker Chapin?"

Reid said, "Would appear he's the dominant half of the kill team, and perhaps responsible for the kidnapping of Kathy Bonder."

"What does Garcia say?"

"Prentiss says Garcia is looking into Chapin, right now."

Taking charge, Hotchner said, "We'll leave Gideon to go after the suspect, while the Kansas City team at the Bonders' will handle the ransom . . . and we'll go to the crime scene."

Supervisory Special Agent Jason Gideon and Supervisory Special Agent Emily Prentiss sat at a table well apart from the local law enforcement activity at the student union.

When they'd found the note, and Kathy Bonder's cell phone, Detective Warren immediately got campus security to lock the building down. Everyone who was in the union when the doors were shuttered had to present ID to get out.

The campus police took names of twelve different Davids, but Abby Querin couldn't come up with any more information . . . and a student having the first name of David (with zero description to fit said student to) didn't really qualify as probable cause to hold anyone.

Already the crime scene team had dusted

the phone and the note for fingerprints. They had started working on tracing all the numbers in the phone's memory, and were dusting the table and chair for prints.

Abby had asked to leave, so she could attend her next class. The young woman had been with them pretty much throughout, and Gideon did not see how she could have been the one to plant the phone, so he acquiesced.

A crime scene analyst brought the note over in a sealed plastic evidence bag and placed it on the table between Gideon and Prentiss.

68,000 IN SMALL, UNMARKED BILLS PLACED IN A NEW SUITCASE. BROKEN ARROW PARK. MIDNIGHT. MORE INSTRUCTIONS LATER. FAILURE TO MEET DEMANDS — SHE DIES! YOU'RE LATE — SHE DIES! ANY COPS — SHE DIES!

Gideon read the note a second time. His eyes went to Prentiss; his words were uninflected: "What do you see?"

"No pronouns concerning the kidnapper?"

"Or *kidnappers,*" Gideon affirmed.

"Do you think the killing duo are also Kathy's abductors?"

"If they are, one thing in this note rings true — she dies if we don't get to her first."

Detective Warren stopped by the table. "Crime scene team's not getting anywhere much — how about you?"

"If the same UnSubs indeed committed the kidnapping," Gideon said, "they are starting to feel invincible. One or both came right into the same room we were in, to leave this message. They know we're here and . . ." He shrugged. ". . . that doesn't scare them an iota."

"Isn't that just peachy," Warren said. "We call in the FBI, and the bad guys get more brazen."

Prentiss said, "Actually, that works in our favor."

"How so?" Warren asked, unconvinced.

Gideon said, "These two UnSubs are in their early to mid-twenties. And we are an army with years of experience hunting criminals."

"Well . . . you make a good point."

"Thank you." He smiled gently at her. "But let me elaborate."

"Please do."

He began to rub his hands together. "The UnSubs are driven by the compulsion of the dominant one, whatever that is. *We* are driven by intellect. Their compulsion is going to take over their lives, and will be the only thing they think about. We will work in shifts, get regular rest, and have a lot more brain power on our side than they have on theirs. They will think they can literally get away with murder, and out of such brazenness carelessness is born; we know we won't let them get away with murder, and will continue to take extreme care. You tell me, Detective — which side would you bet on?"

Warren smiled a little, and her smile was hardly her worst attribute; Gideon figured encouraging her to do so more often was not a bad goal.

"Is that a speech you give all the time to the local hicks?" she asked, still smiling. "Something you recycle all the time?"

"No," he said, guilelessly. "And you people are anything but hicks."

"We needed your help."

"Everyone needs help. That's the human condition."

Getting back on point, Prentiss said, "Gideon's right, but let's not figure these Un-Subs are going to give themselves up, or turn totally stupid. We have advantages, but they're still dangerous, and smart, as Un-Subs go; we need to stop them before they hurt anyone else."

Gideon asked the detective, "Broken Arrow Park? Where is it?"

"South edge of town," Warren said.

Gideon turned to Prentiss. "Where did Reid say this new body was found?"

"In some woods, north of town."

Warren frowned. "Are they trying to split us up? Send us running here and there?"

"Possibly," Gideon said. "But I don't think they thought the body would be found this early in the day. Already, their plans are going awry. . . ."

Gideon's phone chirped and he answered.

"Me, sir," Garcia said. "I've got an address for Becker Chapin."

"One second," he said, and got his notebook and pen out, said, "Go," and she gave it to him.

"Thank you," he said. "Anything else?"

"Well, he's got a sealed juvenile file."

"How sealed?"

"Ummm . . . not *that* sealed. Hypothetically, I could have already opened it."

"Hypothetically, what does it say?"

"Chapin was arrested for arson when he was fourteen."

"Here in Lawrence?"

"Yes, but that's not the best part: he was arrested with an accomplice. David Yarno."

Gideon grinned. "Garcia, right now you are my favorite person in the world. Tell me you have an address for Yarno, too."

"You can promote me to favorite person in the universe, then. Because here it is. . . ."

If Garcia's cheerfulness — and the anime toys with which she surrounded her work station — were defense mechanisms against the horrors that regularly rolled across her monitor screens, she was nonetheless superior at her job, and her upbeat attitude rubbed off on others, including Gideon.

She gave him the address. This one was longer than the first and included a "lot number."

"Lot number?" Gideon asked.

"Trailer park," an eavesdropping Warren whispered, before Garcia could answer.

Garcia said, "Yarno lives with a single mom. Parents divorced when he was eleven. He's an only child. Mom works in a factory that makes tractor seats."

"What about Chapin?"

"Parents still together, though it's unclear whether Chapin lives with them or not. Also an only child. Dad's a mechanic with his own business, mom works as a secretary for an insurance agency. Both guys barely finished high school and wouldn't have been accepted at anyplace other than a land-grant state school."

"Thanks, Garcia. First-rate work."

"Thank you, sir," she said.

And she was gone.

Supervisory Special Agent Derek Morgan pulled the SUV to a stop behind Learman's Crown Vic, off to the side of a dirt road that was little more than a cowpath into the woods.

Squad cars lined each side of the lane, and an ambulance sat on the left behind two of them. A blue Saab was parked ahead of the police cars on the right. The cops were setting up a perimeter around the body and interviewing the two men who'd found the body, while the EMTs were making sure the victim was dead. Once they were satisfied, they backed off and the crime scene unit got started, first snapping photos.

Reid followed Learman, Hotchner, and Morgan over to the body.

This was their freshest crime scene and, at the rate the killers were devolving, the chances of finding usable evidence increased exponentially. Morgan figured they had a good idea of who they were after, by now, but that didn't necessarily translate into a conviction.

Not only were they trying to help the Lawrence PD catch these killers, the BAU team also wanted to make sure twelve licensed drivers would agree that the right people had been arrested and needed to go to prison for a very long time.

The body rested in a weedy area maybe ten yards off a trail leading deeper into the forest. The victim was a young man, maybe twenty at the outside — heavyset and dressed in a generic navy blue policeman's uniform. The badge he wore was obviously flimsy and phony — a cheap toy.

"Motherfucker," Learman muttered. "Thumbing their noses at us! Piss me *off!*"

Hotchner's voice was quiet, cool. "Probably just the reaction they were looking for."

"What?" Learman snapped.

Morgan said, "If these two UnSubs manage to 'piss us off,' we'll lose focus."

Hotchner said, "Concentration is diluted by emotion. If we're angry, we make their job easier."

For a moment Learman seemed to want to argue, albeit more out of frustration with the killers than anything Hotchner or Morgan had said. Then he literally swallowed his anger. "You're right."

"It's not like the victim was a real officer," Hotchner reminded Learman. "This is part of their role-playing. The film they're making."

Morgan said, "Not a cop, just another

homeless person . . . but a person. Who deserves our respect, and our best effort."

"Understood," Learman said, his professional demeanor restored. "We treat him like he's one of ours."

"In the greater sense," Hotchner said, "each of these victims is 'one of ours.'"

"Amen," Morgan said.

The young man lay on his back, arms splayed wide, legs only slightly apart. The thing that jumped out at Morgan was the young man's bruise-covered face: he'd obviously been beaten, his nose broken; poor guy had been punched repeatedly.

This was an escalation in the violence from the previous victims. Though the other victims had all been stabbed repeatedly, and had their throats cut, none had been beaten — until now.

"They're getting more personal," Reid observed.

"We have *got* to stop these guys," Morgan said, hands on hips. "They're ramping up with each kill."

After getting the okay from the crime scene analysts, Learman knelt and turned the body over. The navy blue shirt was soaked black with blood, large areas of pale white skin visible through shredded material that indicated the killer had hacked repeatedly at the victim's back.

"God," Learman said, voice cracking, "they tortured the poor bastard."

Morgan put a hand on the detective's shoulder. "You okay, man?"

Learman breathed in and out, then nodded. "I am really tired of these sons of bitches making us look like we just got off the short bus. I *can't* let anyone else *die.*"

"You're not the only one working on this," Hotchner reminded him.

Learman got up, shaking his head. "It sure as hell feels that way, every time I see another body."

Morgan didn't know what to say to that; neither, apparently, did Hotch or Reid.

"Sorry," the detective said, looking a little embarrassed. "I don't mean any offense. And I didn't mean that you folks haven't been a big help. I mean, Jesus, we wouldn't know *anything* about these guys, hadn't been for you. But I don't want to see one more body. These people were having a hard enough time already, scrounging our streets for meals and somewhere to sleep — then they get preyed on by these monsters."

"We'll get them," Hotchner said. "We're getting close."

Morgan knew how Learman felt; they all did.

"Now," Hotchner said. "Shall we talk to the hikers who found the body?"

As one, they looked back toward the trail.

Learman squinted. "How in the hell did they ever even *see* it?"

"Not sure," Reid admitted. "It's a ways off the path."

"Kind of a hill there, too," Morgan said.

As the quartet started heading back toward the cars, maneuvering the underbrush, a uniformed officer approached.

"Hey, Rob," the uniform said, addressing Learman.

He was a tall, broad-shouldered ash-blond guy, maybe thirty, with a bucket head and light blue eyes.

"Hey, Mac," Learman said. "What have we got?"

"Two hikers over there are John Richmond and Gary Landau," the uniformed man said, not referring to notes. "Both work at KU. They were out for their morning run, and came across the body."

Learman introduced the team to Officer Scot McKenzie. "He's going to be a detective soon. You ever have to come back to Lawrence, you might be dealing with him."

Shaking hands with the young officer, Hotchner said, "Nice to meet you — but we all know you never want to see any of us again."

"Why would that be?" McKenzie asked innocently.

"We're the mean dog in the backyard," Morgan said. "When everything's cool, nobody wants us around; but when serious trouble shows, we get let off our leash."

The two runners both wore shorts, socks and good running shoes. The younger man's T-shirt bore a Dave Matthews Band logo, the older one was in a long-sleeved white tee with blue three-quarter sleeves. Silver hair peeked out from under his KU ball cap. The younger runner wore a navy blue handkerchief as a headband.

"This is Professor John Richmond," Officer McKenzie said, introducing the older runner. Then he added, "And Professor Gary Landau," indicating the younger man.

Learman introduced himself and the FBI agents. They all exchanged handshakes and nods.

Hotchner said, "Tell us what happened."

The two runners glanced at each other, then, surprisingly, the older professor deferred to the younger one. "We run out here every morning. It's quiet, out of the way."

Hotchner nodded.

"We didn't notice anything unusual.

Beautiful sunny spring morning — wish they were all like this . . . except for . . . On the way back, I had to take a leak. If I hadn't, we'd never have seen him there. I know it's probably against the law, urinate in a public park, but I had an extra cup of coffee and —"

Morgan said, good-naturedly, "As long as you didn't urinate across a state line, the FBI has no problem. Please go on."

Landau laughed nervously. "Yeah. Well, I went up to one of the trees, and was just getting ready when I looked down and saw the guy's hand. I followed his arm up to his face, and, well, if you'll pardon the expression, it scared the shit out of me."

Let alone the piss, Morgan thought.

Landau was saying, "So I ran back to the car to call 911. I always leave my cell in the car, before I go running."

"This is just to make sure we don't mix your DNA in with evidence," Hotchner said. "But we need to know, where did you urinate?"

The professor shook his head. "I was scared so badly, I never went."

Once again my profile is spot on, Morgan thought wryly.

"Matter of fact," Landau said, "I've got to go like a racehorse now."

Learman gave the man the blessing of the Lawrence PD to pee, sending the professor well shy of the crime scene.

They all waited for him to disappear into the trees before they laughed. Breaking the tension at crime scenes was as welcome as the relief Professor Landau would be availing himself of about now.

Still, they had another body and the clock was obviously ticking. This duo of killers was beginning to think they were invulnerable. Morgan and the rest of the BAU team needed to prove them wrong.

And soon.

Gideon, Prentiss and Warren pulled up in front of a one-story ranch-style house in a neighborhood that had likely been nice ten or fifteen years ago.

A faded green, the Chapin home had a one-car attached garage and a navy blue five-year-old Ford F-150 in the driveway, a silver toolbox in the cab. A cherry tree, maybe ten feet tall, was the only adornment to an otherwise scruffy, nondescript yard.

The curtains were drawn on the three windows in front. A slightly bigger window at right was probably the living room, the other two bedroom windows, possibly.

Prentiss had used her camera-phone to

take a photo of the note, forwarding it to Garcia, who sent it on to Minet and Parker at the Bonder home. Gideon had phoned to make sure they were getting the ransom together, in case he and Prentiss failed to apprehend Chapin at the parents' home.

On the way over, Warren had radioed for the crime scene team and a SWAT team backup. While they waited for SWAT, the two FBI agents and the local detective retrieved bulletproof vests from the trunk. Gideon and Prentiss slipped FBI windbreakers over the kevlar; Warren's had Lawrence PD stamped on the back and both sleeves. All three checked their pistols. They all wanted this to go peacefully, but if it didn't, they'd be ready.

Five minutes later, both the crime scene van and the SWAT panel truck pulled up and parked. The crime scene team sat tight while the troops piled out of the SWAT vehicle; their captain — a tall, rugged, redheaded, freckle-faced guy named Bruno — assigned them to surround the house.

Gideon advised Warren that they try to go in soft, which meant knocking at the front door . . . as opposed to Captain Bruno's idea of going in hard, meaning tear gas grenades and battering down both the doors.

"We have no reason to believe Kathy Bonder may be in there," Gideon said. "Preemptive SWAT team tactics could get your city sued back to the Stone Age."

Bruno squinted in the shade of his SWAT cap's visor. He was a formidable man with a grim countenance that the Howdy Doody freckles only slightly undercut. "What if she *is* in there?"

"Going in hard could get her killed," Gideon said. "Let us try."

Bruno turned to the local representative. "That how you want it, Detective Warren?"

"It is."

Bruno turned back to Gideon. "First sign of trouble, I'm giving the word."

"I hope you do."

The SWAT commander hung back in the yard as Warren led the way up the steps to the front porch, Gideon and Prentiss right behind her.

Gideon was suddenly aware of how warm the day had become, sweat running down his back under the kevlar. He drew his pistol, his thumb on the safety as he held the weapon's barrel down along the length of his leg, out of sight to whoever might answer the door. Prentiss had her weapon out, too, holding it the same way, slightly behind him to his right. In the lead, Warren had her weapon out and loosely at her side, as well.

Top of the stairs, Warren went to the right side of the front door, Gideon to the left, and Prentiss slid even farther right than Warren, glancing toward the curtained living room window.

After making eye contact with both profilers, Warren took in a deep breath, centered herself, and let it out, then knocked on the screen door.

"Lawrence Police Department," she announced firmly.

For a tense second they waited . . .

. . . nothing.

Another second, a third, fourth — still nothing.

Warren knocked again, louder. "*Lawrence PD!* Anyone home?"

Again, they waited, Gideon straining to hear movement within the house, aware of everything now, every nerve ending on alert. He felt the breeze waft across his face, heard the rustle of leaves on the straggly fruit tree in the yard. The pistol felt lead-weight heavy in his hand. He had it pointed up, now, and reminded himself that if things went south, he would have to step around the screen door, which would open toward him.

Seconds crept glacially by.

A third time, Warren pounded on the door. *"Lawrence Police Department! Last chance! We have a warrant — we'll break down the door!"*

Despite uniformed officers showing up to cordon off the area, Gideon saw neighbors on a front porch across the street. He tensed as Warren took a half step back, prepared to signal Bruno to have his men bring the battering ram.

The SWAT officers with the ram were two feet from the bottom step when the lock on the inside door clicked, and the knob turned.

In the split second he had, Gideon released the tension in his body and eased back from the door.

The inside door swung open and Gideon saw Prentiss bring her pistol into position and Warren slide back. The SWAT men dropped the ram, which clunked to the sidewalk, as their hands all sprang to their holsters.

A man stepped into the doorway. He was wide-shouldered, wore a sleeveless white undershirt and jeans. Even through the screen, Gideon could see the man had not shaved for two or three days.

"What the fuck?" the man blurted, as he banged the screen open. His eyes were on

261

Gideon, and he never looked in the other direction.

As their reluctant host took a menacing step toward Gideon, Warren slipped behind him, and touched the barrel of the gun against his skull. "Freeze. Lawrence PD."

The man lifted his hands slightly and stood very still. He seemed more amused than scared. He had brown hair clipped short, a not totally unpleasant face above a short neck, and wide shoulders. Probably a football player, once upon a time, Gideon surmised.

Warren asked, "Are you Nick Chapin?"

"Yeah. What's this dog-and-pony show about?"

Gideon said, "Becker Chapin is your son?"

"Yeah, he's my son. Would someone please tell me what the hell . . ."

"Is Becker here, Mr. Chapin?"

The mechanic shook his head. "He don't live here anymore. What the hell did he do *now?*"

"If you calm down," Warren said quietly, "I will lower my weapon, and you can lower your hands. How does that sound?"

"Swell," Chapin said.

Warren backed off and holstered her weapon. "We have a warrant to search your residence, sir."

He turned toward her. "Knock yourself out — I ain't done shit."

Gideon asked, "Is your wife home?"

"Naw, she's at work."

"When was the last time you saw your son?"

They moved to one side of the small porch to make room for two SWAT officers entering the house. Then Gideon, Prentiss, and Warren led Chapin down the steps and into the front yard.

"We ain't seen him since the first of the year," Chapin said, "and before that, he wasn't around much. Not since he hooked up with that Yarno kid, back in junior high? That's when he changed. Back then, I tried talkin' to him; so did his mother. We didn't get to square fucking one with him. He tuned us out and tuned in to whatever shit this Yarno yahoo was peddlin'."

Gideon asked, "Then how did he wind up giving college a go?"

"Film school," Chapin said. "Pure and simple. If KU hadn't had a film school, who knows what kind of trouble that boy would get into? . . . Only, uh, judgin' by the Fourth of July cop parade around my house, little dipshit musta got himself in deep, this time. You gonna tell me what?"

Gently, Gideon said, "Have you seen the

news reports about the homeless people being murdered, Mr. Chapin?"

And Chapin seemed immediately to know what his boy was capable of.

He closed his eyes, lowered his head, and pressed the fingers of his left hand into his forehead as if he could somehow will, or perhaps massage, this terrible news away.

They backed off their questioning, letting him come to grips with it.

The two SWAT team members came out of the house, bounced down the stairs, then moved over to Captain Bruno to report that the house was clear. Malone and his crime scene team went in.

Finally, after what seemed a herculean effort, Becker Chapin's father raised his teary eyes to them. "You . . . you told my wife yet?"

"No," Gideon said. "You were our first stop."

"We'll see her next," Warren added.

"Please," Chapin said, pathetically, "let me go with you! This . . . aw, God, this is gonna kill her, just fuckin' *kill* her. . . ."

Gideon did his best not to show any reaction to Chapin's choice of verbs. "We'd prefer you be with us. Might soften the blow." He didn't mention that with both Chapins in view of Prentiss, Warren and himself, the parents would have no chance to warn their son.

Chapin was saying, "I just want to be with my wife."

"Not a problem," Warren said.

Shaking his head, sobbing now, Chapin said, "I swear to you people, we did the best we could. . . ." Then he sat down, clumsily and hard, on the lawn, and buried his face in his hands.

Before long, Captain Malone from the crime scene team exited the house and marched down the stairs to join them in the yard. He gave Gideon a little nod, then moved off a ways from the father.

Gideon and Prentiss joined the crime scene analyst as Warren stayed with Chapin.

"Sonny boy's not there," Malone said. "There's stuff in his room, and we'll take it into evidence; but it doesn't look like he's been around for a while. There's a monitor, a printer, and some cords, but the computer's gone. My guess is, it was a laptop and the kid took it with him."

"Thanks," Gideon said. "All right if we go in?"

"All yours."

Gideon and Prentiss climbed the stairs. Inside, Gideon stopped, letting his eyes adjust to the dark interior. The living room was neat, but the furniture was worn and tired. The whole room had an atrophied feel about it, dingy white with a yellowish tan ceiling from years of smoking. Next to a well-used recliner in the corner, cigarette butts swarmed an ashtray and a beer can rested on a cork coaster atop a small round end table.

They looked into a tiny kitchen with a small dining room off that, reminding Gideon of a few thousand homes he had been in over the last thirty years, too often houses that seemed to sag under the weight of tragedies. Was there enough paint in the world to cover the stain of their pain?

A short hallway led back to the bathroom and three bedrooms. The bath and the master were on the right, a spare room first on the left, then Becker's room. Three members of the crime scene team were packing up items in evidence bags and boxes. They looked like a Tyvek-suited moving crew.

Gideon and Prentiss peeked in and saw a bed, a desk that held the computer components Malone had mentioned, and a huge wooden cable spool, laid flat like a table, serving as a stand for a nineteen-inch tube TV, a DVD player, and shelf sound system.

Horror film and heavy metal band posters

adorned the walls, and above the slim twin bed, tacked carefully to the ceiling so it looked down on the occupant, was a movie poster that showed a beautiful blonde who strikingly resembled Kathy Bonder.

The blonde looked terrified, a huge butcher knife hanging over her head, a literal sword of Damocles. In red blood-dripping letters were the words *Il Morte Improvviso . . .*

. . . and Gideon knew they had indeed identified one half of their killing duo.

He indicated the poster.

Prentiss nodded. "The movie Garcia told us about."

Within Becker's room, Gideon picked a framed photo up off the computer desk, and two boys peered out at him. They were teenagers, both wearing black T-shirts touting heavy metal bands, and raggedy jeans. They wore their hair long, the taller one — blond with broad shoulders — had a ready smile, though his eyes were oddly wary, as if suspicious of the camera lens itself.

The smaller one had darker, longer hair with blond highlights, and seemed younger than the blond boy. He had big bland brown eyes and a thin-lipped mouth.

Gideon took the photo out and showed it to Mr. Chapin.

"That's Becker," Chapin acknowledged with a nod, pointing to the blond boy. Pointing at the other boy, he said, "And that's that shit, David Yarno."

At last, Gideon knew who his UnSubs were.

He was sure the BAU team had identified the right perps and even more certain he was looking into their faces in the photo.

He checked his watch — already after noon.

"We've got to get this photo to Hotch and the others," he told Prentiss and Warren. "Kathy Bonder's got less than twelve hours before her first starring film role becomes her final one."

CHAPTER NINE

The crime scene team found no sign of tripod marks in the woods around the new body. They had, however, discovered a number of sets of footprints, two belonging to the pair of KU professors, and another to the police-uniformed victim. This still left at least two more sets that could be the killers'.

On the ride back to town, Supervisory Special Agent Derek Morgan drove, with Hotchner next to him and Reid in back, as they followed Learman's Crown Vic. They'd barely got started when Gideon called and spoke to Hotch.

Morgan had learned long ago not to try to follow the taciturn Hotch's side of a phone conversation. When the supervisory agent slipped his phone away, Morgan glanced at him with an unspoken question.

"Becker Chapin and David Yarno," Hotchner said.

Eyes back on Learman's vehicle as they traversed the slightly twisty two-lane wooded road, Morgan asked, "Our Un-Subs?"

"They were. Now they're our suspects."

Like a kid in the backseat, Reid leaned forward as much as his seat belt would allow. "In custody?"

"Is it ever that easy?" Hotchner said.

"Well," Reid said, "on occasion —"

Morgan said, "Reid — please don't answer the rhetorical questions. It makes my head hurt."

Hotchner ignored this, and said, "Gideon and Prentiss just left the Chapin house, where they found out Becker doesn't live with his parents anymore. They're on their way to talk to Becker's mother now."

Reid asked Hotchner, "How did Gideon move Chapin and Yarno from the UnSub column into Suspect?"

"Everything is starting to point to them," Hotchner said. "When Gideon and Prentiss went to the parents' home, and checked out Chapin's room? They found the poster from that Italian movie. . . ."

"*Il Morte Improvviso,*" Reid volunteered.

"Yes. Poster was on the ceiling of Chapin's bedroom, starring an actress strongly resembling Kathy Bonder."

270

"Whoa," Morgan said. "So we *are* working one case. What about this Yarno character?"

Hotchner's shrug was barely perceptible. "My guess is Learman's getting the same call we're getting, and will lead us to Yarno's. We'll try to nail that half of the team, at least."

From the back came Reid's voice again: "Does Gideon have any sense of which is the dominant one?"

"Chapin's the director of the movie," Hotchner said matter-of-factly. "Makes sense that he'd be the dominant partner."

"Can a director be directed?" Reid asked.

Morgan said, "It's possible, but —"

"That was a rhetorical question," Reid said, and grinned impishly at Morgan in the rearview mirror, who chuckled, shaking his head.

Learman turned onto a four-lane street, still thick with trees, and headed west. Morgan didn't know where they were, but this confirmed Hotchner's read of the situation — they were not heading back to the Law Enforcement Center.

Morgan would just stay on the cop's tail. After about two miles, Learman took a left, then a right, and another left. They were out of the woods, literally if not figuratively, the lush green surroundings of the park replaced by the stark squalor of a low-end trailer court, the short streets crowded with mobile home after mobile home. Some were newer and nicely kept-up, these almost invariably with retired folks sitting out front on well-maintained little lawns; but most appeared older, and less well maintained.

Learman drew slowly to a stop next to a trailer with a yellow Honda parked on the gravel driveway next to it. Morgan parked behind the detective. At Hotchner's prompt, they all donned bulletproof vests, and had barely finished the process when the SWAT backup team showed up with another crime scene crew.

Gideon had passed along the info that Yarno lived in a single-parent residence with his factory worker mother. Hotchner was first up the two aluminum stairs to the door, Morgan right behind him, Reid and Learman bringing up the rear, the SWAT team hanging back, though they had the trailer surrounded.

No weapons were drawn, but Morgan and Reid had their hands on gun butts.

Hotchner knocked on the door and a moment or two later a woman pushed it open. From where he stood, Morgan could see her well: five-three and probably one hundred pounds, in a short-sleeve pink sweat-shirt with a kitten on it, and blue jeans and tennies; her brown hair had a reddish tinge and her blue-gray eyes a certain weariness.

She smiled at Hotchner, as if the sight of armed men in kevlar vests was a mildly amusing diversion in a boring life.

"Be of help?"

"FBI, Ms. Yarno," Hotchner said, displaying his ID. "Is David here?"

The smile faded, along with any sense that these officers were mistaken coming around here to see a harmless nonentity like herself, as certain dots were connected. "Tell me it isn't . . . What's he *done?*"

"Is David here?"

She shook her head. "No. No, not since . . . last fall, I guess."

"You haven't seen him at all since then?"

"Now and then," she said. "He stops by. But he hasn't lived here in ages. What's going on?"

The crime scene team leader, Lieutenant Ludke, an older plainclothes officer, had picked up the search warrant from the courthouse on the way to the Yarno trailer. He stepped forward and handed the warrant to Morgan, who passed it on to Hotchner, who ended the relay action with Ms. Yarno.

"Would you step outside, please, ma'am?" Hotchner asked. "We can talk out here while these officers proceed."

Morgan noted Hotchner's careful phrasing: he had not said "crime scene analysts," because of the alarm that might impart.

"Please," she said, her voice ragged with worry, "tell me what's going on."

"Mrs. Yarno, you must be familiar with this string of murdered homeless people in Lawrence."

"Oh, God, David's *dead?*"

This reaction took them all by surprise. Even Hotchner seemed to back up a little. "Um . . . no, ma'am. He's a person of interest."

Again, Morgan noted the careful choice of words: "person of interest," not "suspect." You had to hand it to Hotch. . . .

Still, the suspect's mother's demeanor changed instantly from devastated to at least mistrustful, if not downright angry. "You think *David's* involved in those?" she asked, already shaking her head. "That's stupid. That's just silly."

She moved outside, though, perching on the top step.

Amping it up, Hotchner said, "The evidence indicates that he and his friend Becker Chapin may be involved —"

"If anybody's killing anybody," she cut in, "it's that little bastard Becker Chapin."

"Ma'am . . . if you'll just move down off the steps . . ."

They got out of the way of the SWAT team moving around them and into the trailer. The crime scene crew edged slightly closer, but no one would be doing much of anything until SWAT declared the mobile home clear.

"What you say may well be possible," Hotchner said to her. "We have more evidence implicating Becker Chapin than your son. All we want to find out is the truth, and if it clears David, we'll be delighted."

Well, Morgan thought, *maybe not* delighted. . . .

Ms. Yarno said, "The truth? Truth is that that little Chapin creep turned my boy against me. Before we moved here, David was a good boy, a fine son, even after the divorce."

Morgan, watching from a step away, was marveling at the ease with which his supervisor had led the distraught mother into talking about her son, even to the point of giving something away.

"Divorce?" Hotchner asked.

"When David was in sixth grade, Donnie and me split. David was eleven. His father used to hit me, and when David tried to get in between, Donnie hit David, too. So I got a divorce, and a restraining order, and we moved here."

The SWAT team came out and pronounced the mobile home clear. The crime scene crew entered and got to work.

"Moved here from where?" Hotchner asked.

"Liberal," she said.

Morgan's eyebrows rose — couldn't help themselves. "Liberal? There's a town called Liberal, Kansas?"

She nodded distractedly. "Southwest corner of the state."

After flicking Morgan the tiniest of irritated glances, Hotchner asked her, "How did you get from Liberal to Lawrence?"

"I got a cousin who's a supervisor at Robbins Manufacturing — Johnny Dryden. He landed me on as a third shift assembler. They make tractor seats."

Hotchner provided an encouraging nod.

"Decent enough money," she said, "but that meant David had to grow up fast. Maybe too fast. I mean, it was just the two of us."

Hotchner frowned sympathetically. "How long ago was that?"

"Ten years," she said. "I could've gone to

second shift, I suppose; but I figured it was more important for me to be here. When David got home from school every day? He was always a good boy."

"Tell us about him," Hotchner said.

Suddenly she seemed to discern the garden path Hotchner was leading her down, and shook her head. "I shouldn't even be talking to you at all."

"You said your son was a good boy. If you can help us prove him innocent, you should."

She nodded but said nothing, her expression suspicious.

"We need to understand David," Hotchner said. "And you could help us. Who would know him better than his own mother?"

That seemed to mollify her, and she said, "David was always kind of small for his age. He was bright . . . *very* bright . . . but he was always small. I was afraid his father would start beating him as he got older."

"You said your ex-husband *did* hit your son. . . ."

"Not at first. He slapped David a few times, but I made it clear to Donald, that's my ex, that if he ever beat on David again, I would kill him."

"He believed you?"

"He must have. After that, he didn't touch David. But then when David got a little older, and started grabbing at Donnie, when he was hitting me? Donnie forgot all about my threats. He was drunk and mad and he just didn't give two shits. That last time? Son of a bitch broke my goddamn shoulder, twisting my arm behind my back."

Hotchner's mouth twitched. "What happened then?"

"I went to the hospital, they called the cops, and DFS came in and got David."

"That's when you divorced Donald Yarno and moved here."

"Yes," Ms. Yarno said. "But it was tough on David. He lost a parent. Even though Donnie was a crawling piece of shit, he was David's dad. Poor little guy moved to a new town, where he didn't know a single person, except me . . . and moms don't count, do they? Then, to top it off, he's moving from elementary school to junior high. My cousin Johnny tried to help, took him fishing, stuff like that. But David didn't really have any friends. That's awfully hard for a boy in junior high. I'm lucky he come through it as well as he done."

Morgan kept his face neutral, but he was thinking she wasn't lucky at all; her son's experiences had helped send him down the road to a psychosis whose last stop was serial killer.

"Junior high," Hotch was saying. "That was where David met Becker Chapin?"

"Yes. At first, I thought Becker was good for David. I mean, finally David had a friend! When we first moved here, David got bullied by some older boys. Having a friend who was bigger? That made life easier for David. Becker put a stop to the bullying. So, at first, I suppose you'd have to say I liked him."

"What changed your mind?"

She shrugged.

She was clamming up again. Morgan knew the woman was hiding something, something about her son.

When Hotch had gotten off the phone, he'd told Morgan and Reid that Garcia had gotten David's name from Chapin's sealed juvenile file . . . and Morgan could only wonder if that was what Ms. Yarno wanted to keep quiet about now.

Hotchner would get to that, of course; the only question was whether he'd attack directly or circumvent the issue, and sneak up on it.

"May I ask a personal question?" Hotchner said. Then without waiting for permission, he asked, "Did David have trouble with enuresis after the age of twelve?"

"In your what?" Ms. Yarno asked.

"Bed-wetting."

She seemed vaguely embarrassed. "Yes, but that was just because of all the pressures David was under that I already told you about."

"Was David ever cruel to small animals?"

"Cruel?"

Reid stepped into the conversation now. "Dissection, setting them on fire, skinning them?"

Morgan could never quite get used to Reid reeling off such lists of atrocities as if ordering a burger, fries and Coke.

Maggie Yarno was shaking her head now. "No, no. Nothing like that! He's a good boy."

Hotchner said, "David showed an interest in science. Sometimes boys interested in science do biological experiments on animals."

"In school, you mean?"

"No. On their own."

Hotchner had said this, Morgan noted, as if he were applauding the boy's initiative.

"He did do some . . . experiments like that," she said. "And I complained about it. Said it wasn't . . . nice, but David said without animal experimentation, we wouldn't have medicine, or perfume. And he was always going on about studying science in college."

"Did he ever attend college?" Hotchner asked.

"He was getting ready to when he moved out. David still hasn't settled on a career, just yet."

Unfortunately, Morgan thought, David Yarno had indeed chosen a career of sorts.

"Mrs. Yarno," Hotchner said, shifting gears, "we already know that David was arrested with Becker Chapin for arson, when they were fourteen."

She paled. "No . . . no that's not true. . . ."

"It is true."

"But it's not possible. How . . . how could you . . . know that? That record's *sealed.*"

"We're the FBI," Hotchner said as if that explained it, and maybe it did. "Fire starting, cruelty to animals, bed wetting, are the three factors that make up what profilers call the homicidal triad."

Mrs. Yarno just stared at them, her surprise possibly mirroring that of her son's other victims when that first blow came out of nowhere.

Supervisory Special Agent Emily Prentiss was back at the Law Enforcement Center, as were Gideon and Detective Warren, all seated again at the big table in the conference room.

Nick Chapin and his wife, Danielle, were cloistered in an interview room with cups of coffee, a box of tissues, and — despite the Lawrence PD's rule against it — an ashtray for Mr. Chapin.

Prentiss had just looked in on them, even though a uniformed officer was posted outside the door and a detective watched them through the two-way glass.

She checked her watch: well after two p.m., less than ten hours until the ransom deadline for Kathy Bonder. Jareau was back at the Bonder home with SAs Parker and Minet, working that end, while Hotchner, Morgan and Reid were off searching the home of the alleged partner, David Yarno.

A uniformed officer brought Warren a folder.

Gideon asked, "What do you have there?"

"Latest victim has been identified," Warren said. "The young man in the woods, dressed like a policeman?"

He nodded.

"Benjamin Gray, a former KU student," Warren continued. "Crime scene people got his prints from the body, ran them through AFIS, got a hit."

Gideon frowned. "College kid with a

record?"

"Right after school started last fall, he was one of several underage kids picked up for drinking at a frat party. They all paid a small fine, but that was it. That got us his fingerprints."

"He was a student at KU when he was arrested?" Gideon asked. "But not when he was killed?"

"Hardly unheard of around here," Warren said, "for a kid to flunk out, not tell his parents, and live on the streets till getting his act together. Only, of course, he didn't."

Gideon drew in a breath, let it out. "We need to find out a couple of things."

Warren's eyebrows rose above her glasses. "For instance?"

Prentiss picked up: "Whether there's a school connection between Chapin and Gray. Or a connection between Gray and Yarno, somehow."

"Okay," Warren said, considering that. "Anything else?"

Gideon said, "If Chapin knew Gray at college — and targeted an acquaintance, not just another homeless victim — that's one more indication that Kathy Bonder is in serious danger."

Warren said, "I'll get on the phone right away," and headed off to her desk.

"I'll call Garcia," Prentiss said, getting out her cell. "Maybe she's had some luck finding something identifiable in that video."

"Do that," Gideon said. "Meantime, I'll talk to the Chapins again. They may have an idea where their son is, and either aren't telling us, or don't *know* that they know."

That confused Prentiss, but she let it go, asking instead, "Either way, how are you going to get them to tell you what we need?"

"Step one," Gideon said, "get them talking. The rest will, hopefully, fall into line."

He looked up at the wall clock.

Prentiss followed his eyes up to the LED numbers — 2:53.

Neither profiler said anything.

Neither had to.

The crime scene team exited the Yarno mobile home. They knew precious little more than they had when they entered.

Reid and Morgan went in.

The living room was tiny but neat: couch opposite the door, with a single end table. An easy chair rested against the near wall. The galley kitchen, with a small, round table and two chairs, was to the right. A hallway to the left ran the length of the place.

Leading Reid into the hall, Morgan could

see the master bedroom through an open door at the end of the hallway that included two doors on the right. The first was what had been David's bedroom before he moved out.

In his present living quarters, Morgan had a walk-in closet bigger than this bedroom; but growing up, he'd had friends who lived in rooms like this — some had even had to share them. A twin bed sat against the right-hand wall under three shelves, each about three feet long. The crime scene team had cleared them, so Morgan could only guess they'd held books.

A minuscule desk resided against the far wall, a few peripherals still here, but clearly David had taken his computer when he split.

"If they're not living with their parents," Reid asked, "where are they?"

"Now that's a very good question," Morgan said. "Not at all rhetorical."

Obviously, the kid had taken the stuff from his bedroom that was important to him, and moved it — where? Both young men had cell phones, but they hadn't been turned on in months, had probably ditched them in favor of impossible to track prepaid ones. The Chapin kid had a van, but the BOLO (Be-On-the-Look-Out for) had turned up nothing.

While Reid stayed in the hall, Morgan went over the tiny bedroom. To his left, each sliding door on the minuscule closet displayed small versions of posters for various horror movies. A larger-size movie poster, over the bed — *Suspiria* — adorned the wall next to the shelving.

Morgan opened the closet and found gaps in the hanging clothes where David had gathered things on moving out, unless the crime scene team had taken them into evidence; he'd find out later.

Absently, he shifted some of the hangers, reading the T-shirts that hung on them. His finger got caught in a wire hanger and tipped it off the rod, sending it to the floor. He knelt and grabbed the hanger but its hook caught in the cheap carpeting, pulling up one corner.

All he'd wanted to do was read a T-shirt or two, to gauge where this kid was coming from; and now he was on his hands and knees, wrestling with a hanger and a piece of torn carpeting. . . .

How bad could this day get?

Another rhetorical question.

Then, as he tried to free the hanger, the carpet drew back, revealing the dark corner of wooden flooring beneath it, where Morgan thought he saw something odd. He jerked the hanger free and the carpeting fell. Grabbing a corner, he lifted and yanked it back — too dark for him to see the floor beneath clearly.

"Reid, get a flashlight and shine it in here!"

"Find something?"

"Get the flashlight and I'll know."

Reid returned in less than a minute. He leaned in over Morgan, shining the beam down onto the floor.

"What is it?" he asked.

Now that he could see better, Morgan could make out hinges.

"A trapdoor," Morgan said. "Get Hotch and the crime scene guys."

Forty-five minutes later, the crime scene analysts reported that the trapdoor had been used by David to sneak in and out of his mother's mobile home — judging by the footprints underneath, the last time had been recently.

A loose aluminum apron piece on the far side, under the structure, had served as a doorway, David crawling up through the trapdoor to get in. No trailer was positioned on the side where the loose apron piece was, only a sparsely wooded area.

When Hotchner told Ms. Yarno about the

trapdoor, she said she'd had no idea it existed.

Hotchner said, "He's used it recently."

She shrugged. "Why would he? He's got a key to the place."

"Maybe he didn't want to be seen."

Mrs. Yarno shrugged and threw up her hands.

A crime scene analyst came around the corner of the mobile home, holding a plastic evidence bag, which he handed to Hotchner. All three BAU team members gathered around to see what was in the bag.

A photograph — a Polaroid to be exact. Of Chapin and Yarno in front of a dilapidated trailer in the woods. Morgan glanced around, but the scraggly trees around the mobile home park were not a match.

Hotchner held up the photo to Ms. Yarno. "Where was this taken?"

Her eyes widened. "*I* don't know. How should I?"

Lying, Morgan thought.

Learman, who had been hovering on the sidelines, stepped forward now. "Let me have a look."

Showing him the photo, Hotchner asked, "Familiar in any way?"

"Nope. Just an old trailer somebody dragged out into the woods, maybe to use as a hunting cabin."

"Can we find it?"

Learman stroked his chin. "Lot of places it could be. We can look, but where? Can't even be sure it's local — could be around Clinton Lake or Perry Lake or around Topeka, Leavenworth, Atchison, or, hell, off in Missouri. All easy driving distance."

Morgan said, "You haven't narrowed it down much."

"Maybe you can profile that trailer," Learman said dryly.

"What about me?" Ms. Yarno asked. "Can I go now?"

Learman turned. "Sorry, ma'am, but you'll have to come with us."

She frowned, clearly put out. "What's the charge? What did *I* do?"

"No charge, ma'am. I'll be taking you in as a material witness."

"I want a lawyer!"

"We can get you a public defender, down at the Law Enforcement Center."

Mrs. Yarno stood there trembling with rage and fear, finding nothing else to say. Morgan knew the woman was protecting her son, but it was hard to think ill of her for that — people rarely sold out their own children, even if it was the right thing to do.

Still, he had to try.

He went over to her and said, "Mrs. Yarno, your son and Becker Chapin may be holding a young woman against her will. Her life is very probably in danger. If you could tell us where your son might be, an innocent life might be saved."

"My son wouldn't do that," she said.

"But the Chapin kid might. You don't like him much. Where might we look for him?"

She just shook her head.

Morgan watched Learman load the woman into the backseat of a patrol car.

Not the member of the Yarno family he wanted to see hauled away.

CHAPTER TEN

Less than four hours until the deadline.

The sun was setting both on Lawrence and the BAU team's chances of catching this killing duo before the ransom cutoff passed. Except for Jareau (who was again with the stricken Bonder family) and Hotchner (who was re-interviewing David Yarno's mother), the teammates were all back in the Law Enforcement Center conference room, searching for a way to turn shreds of evidence into something meaningful that could lead them to the killers.

Supervisory Special Agent Jason Gideon took stock of his people: Emily Prentiss sat with her face buried in her laptop; Dr. Spencer Reid pored over statistical analysis; Detective Lucy Warren studied the photo of the two boys in front of the trailer; Derek Morgan read material in a file; and Detective Rob Learman was at the far end of the table, keeping his voice low as he spoke on the phone.

Once the deadline passed without payment, Gideon knew, the girl would die; but, statistically, even if the kidnappers got the money, the girl would also likely die. He was having difficulty developing any scenario in which Kathy Bonder did *not* die. And none came to mind that did not include finding the killers before midnight. Though he hadn't looked at a clock for hours, Gideon knew almost to the second how much time they had left.

Hotchner strode into the conference room carrying a cup of coffee. Around Hotch's eyes a certain haggardness showed, but Gideon admired his team leader's steadiness, the hot steaming liquid in the cup as motionless as a mill pond.

Gideon asked, "Any luck with Ms. Yarno?"

"No," Hotchner said. "How about you with the Chapins?"

"No. Actually, I think they *want* to help; but they have no idea where their son is. Or, for that matter, what he's been up to for the last few months."

Hotchner twitched a humorless smile. "Not so with Yarno's mother — she *knows* something, I can read it . . . but she'll never talk; I can read that, too."

"She and her son are mutual survivors of

an abusive husband/father."

Pacing slowly, not taking a seat at the table, Hotchner nodded gravely. "Right. And she'll do anything to protect him, even the *wrong* thing."

Gideon shrugged. "She's his mother."

Morgan stretched, then bent back down over the report he was reading.

Gideon went over to him. "What have you got here?"

Morgan glanced up. "Geographic profile of the crime scenes."

"Looking for the anchor point?"

"Yup."

Serial offenders, like everyone else on the planet, tended to move and operate in patterns through and around familiar geographic areas, hunting in convenient areas. Those actions would provide a pie-shaped wedge of the city comprising their comfort zone.

Those who believed in geographic profiling — and Gideon knew of a fair number of skeptics — further postulated an eighty percent chance that suspects would live within the wedge, and a fifty percent chance the anchor point would be within the pointy end of that wedge.

Gideon asked, "Any luck?"

Morgan shook his head. "Their hunting

ground is very small — only about a ten- to fifteen-square-block area downtown. We know where they will probably strike next. . . ."

"But," Gideon finished, "it doesn't give us any clue as to where they are *now*."

Morgan nodded glumly.

Learman got off the phone and announced, "SWAT team is setting up in Broken Arrow Park. They're working with the agents at the house, to try and trap our wandering boys at the ransom drop."

"That's fine," Gideon said. "But it's risky."

"You're suggesting they shouldn't —"

"No. I'm suggesting we see if we can find them *before* that." Gideon leaned back in his chair. "There's a nasty possibility we need to face."

Prentiss, who hadn't seemed to be listening, looked up from her laptop screen. "That they may kill the hostage, right before going to pick up the ransom?"

Gideon's nod was perhaps a sixteenth-of-an-inch lowering of his head; but no one in the room missed it.

Reid, frowning, asked, "How big is that park?"

Shrugging, Learman said, "Pretty good size. Couple acres? It's on the south edge of town — lots of woods."

Prentiss asked, "Enough to hide a mobile home?"

"Probably not," the detective said. "People use that park too much. Someone would have seen something."

Gideon tilted his head. "Emily, can we redo the geographic profile, using Broken Arrow Park as the anchor point?"

Her eyebrows hiked. "That will give us a pretty big search area. . . ."

"It's a start," Gideon said. "Their downtown hunting ground is based on availability of targets, not necessarily convenience for the hunters."

"But for the ransom drop," Morgan said, sitting up, eyes brightening, "they'll want an area they're more *comfortable* in . . . since collecting a ransom is a different kind of hunting than they're accustomed to."

"Exactly," Gideon said, and allowed himself a smile. "They're comfortable hunting their homeless victims, because they hunt where the victims are. And they've grown comfortable with the territory, because of that experience."

Hotchner jumped in. "Picking up a ransom at a drop is something new for them. They'll choose a territory where they're more comfortable."

Morgan was nodding. "Collecting the

ransom downtown makes no sense. The homeless victims play no role in the pickup, plus it's a busy area, lots of people, greater chance of being seen, of getting caught."

Hotchner said, "And they are waiting till the last minute, apparently, to let the Bonders know *where* in the park to drop off the ransom."

Meanwhile, Prentiss was jabbing away at the computer keys.

In front of Morgan on the table, his cell phone vibrated and he snatched it up, checked the caller ID, then hit the button. "Talk to me."

"I enhanced the photo you sent me," Garcia said, sounding breathless. "Two boys in front of the trailer?"

"I'm looking at it," he said. A copy of that photo was nearby and he'd already dragged it over.

"See that sign on a post in the corner of the frame? Almost out of shot?"

" 'No trespassing.' "

"That's it. Only there's more smaller lettering underneath."

"Which I can't make out."

"My mojo brought out that lettering; says, 'Dryden's Den.' "

"Oh, hell," Morgan said. "The cousin."

Though she didn't know what he was

referring to, the computer tech went swiftly, professionally onward: "I found a parcel of land on North 700th Road south of Lawrence that's owned by a Jonathon A. Dryden."

Morgan grinned at his cell. "You are the best, angel. And I owe you."

"I am," she said proudly. "And you do."

They clicked off.

All eyes were on Morgan.

"Detective Learman," Morgan said, "you know North 700th Road?"

"Sure."

"Seems Johnny Dryden, Maggie Yarno's cousin, owns a piece of property out there."

The detective frowned. "That's all woods, hunting cabins and fishing holes. . . ."

Gideon said, "Just the sort of environment these killers need."

"And," Morgan said, "the perfect place to stick an old trailer turned 'cabin.'"

Hotchner, the only one already on his feet, said, "Let's go," and the rest were up before he'd completed the two-word sentence.

As they exited the conference room, Hotchner asked Learman, "Will we be able to find this place in the dark?"

"I can get us good and goddamn close," the detective said.

Right behind them, Morgan said, "Don't

worry — Garcia will do the rest."

They were in the parking lot when Warren asked, "What about the SWAT team?"

"No," Gideon said firmly. "We don't want to scare these guys off, or spook them into killing their hostage. *We* do this."

They piled into the two SUVs, and once again Supervisory Special Agent Derek Morgan got behind the wheel, with Learman taking the passenger seat and Reid and Gideon in back. The other SUV Hotchner drove with Prentiss and Warren riding.

Everybody had checked their weapons and donned bulletproof vests before they left the Law Enforcement Center, so there would be no time wasted when they reached the property. Each profiler, and the detectives too, carried a high-intensity flashlight.

Learman guided him to North 700th Road, then Morgan phoned Garcia who used the SUV's GPS to guide them to a dirt road that ran off to the right — an unlighted single lane riddled with divots and potholes.

Morgan killed the headlights and slowed to under five miles per hour, creeping up the path, hoping they could take these killers by surprise. Only a few stars dotted the night sky, a quarter moon providing scant illumination as the Tahoe crawled forward, Hotchner's SUV right behind. Ahead, a clearing could be seen, barely visible through the trees lining the lane; but then Morgan thought he saw the moon glint off something white, and he braked to a slow stop.

They all had earpieces and radios on, and Morgan used his.

"Hotch," Morgan whispered, "the trailer's about twenty yards in front of us."

"Copy that."

They eased out of the SUVs, closing doors slowly and as silently as possible, the interior lights of both vehicles already switched off. Then Morgan led his teammates and the two detectives cautiously ahead, fanning out. Using hand signals, Morgan got everyone spread around the trailer, then he and Hotchner took the lead, edging up to the door.

The interior of the mobile home at first seemed pitch black, but Morgan could tell that the windows were draped with heavy black. A wooden box sat below the door, creating a single huge step.

Morgan nodded for Hotchner to reach up and open the door, indicating he (Morgan) would go in first. Hotchner nodded, as Morgan positioned himself two feet or so away, so that the swing of the door didn't clip him.

Then Hotch reached up, nodded again, and jerked the thing open.

Morgan took one step forward, hit the box with the next step, then catapulted into the mobile home, rolled once on the carpeted floor, and came up on one knee, gun poised, flashlight in his left hand. He swung around in a complete circle and saw . . .

. . . nothing.

He made a quick check of the other rooms; this proved fruitless, as well, although disturbing telltale signs did present themselves, in particular shackles bolted to the floor in the living room.

He keyed the radio.

"Clear," he whispered. "Suspects not here. Bonder girl, either."

"Clear," Hotchner repeated.

Were the killers already on their way to the ransom drop?

Two hours remained before the midnight deadline, and the duo would have only about a ten-minute ride.

Why would they leave so early?

They had a phone call to make, sure, but that could be done anywhere, en route on a cell phone for that matter. Did they have a trap of their own to set? If so — and with

Broken Arrow Park the drop point — the SWAT team would have encountered them already, and Morgan and company would have heard by now.

Something was out of kilter.

Morgan returned to the door, clicked off the flash and shrugged down at Hotchner, who shrugged back.

The other profilers and the two local detectives came back around and convened in front of the funky beat-up trailer. Morgan could clearly see the "No Trespassing" sign with the legend "Dryden's Den."

"We've been one step behind these bastards all the way," Learman said, sotto voce.

"Wherever they are," Morgan said, "they have Kathy Bonder with them."

As they stood in a loose circle, each wondering what their next move should be, a squeal — almost animal, but surely human — cut the night like a blade.

Morgan glanced at Hotch, whose head had turned toward the woods beyond the rear of the trailer. Everyone else was turning that way, too, when a second shriek clawed at the night, this time a full-fledged scream, and Morgan ran toward the sound.

Behind him, he could hear the others thrashing into the woods, but he was way out in front, moving quickly but carefully in the limited light, courtesy of the stars and that chunk of moon. Last thing he (or any of them) needed was to step in a hole or trip over an exposed root. . . .

And as it was, they already sounded like the Seventh Cavalry galloping toward Little Big Horn, an image Morgan immediately hoped was not a portent of the outcome.

Then another scream, a hopeless despairing cry, beckoned from off to his left.

As he turned, Morgan caught a glimpse of a bobbing light of some kind, almost as if a vehicle with a small bright headlight were rumbling over rough ground out there. His gun seemed to jump into his hand, and he was sprinting now, holes and roots and caution be damned. In seconds, the woman (and it *was* a woman) screaming in these woods would be dead, and he would not allow that, not on his watch. . . .

Still, he was not entirely reckless, keeping the flashlight turned off, despite any danger from the underbrush. No point in making himself an easy target.

The others were still behind him, crunching and snapping through the undergrowth, but farther back now.

Then he was at the edge of a small clearing.

He stopped.

Somebody was sprinting toward him out of the darkness.

Morgan raised his gun.

The sprinter had longish blond hair, but Morgan couldn't make out the face, in the limited light, or even any detail about the dark clothing, though it appeared loose and flowing.

Was it one of the killers?

When the approaching runner was perhaps twenty feet away, Morgan yelled, *"FBI! Halt!"*

The figure kept running toward him. When the distance closed to twenty feet, Morgan's finger tightened around the trigger and he centered the bead at the end of the barrel on center mass. . . .

"Help me!"

The voice was high-pitched — *female.*

And, just in time, Morgan realized the blond-haired figure — in what appeared to be a black dress with black leggings and white collar — running toward him was Kathy Bonder; and he lowered his weapon.

She ran into his arms, knocking him backward a couple of steps and he finally saw what was behind her, a black-masked, black-clothed figure, sprinting across the clearing toward them — the bright light bobbling behind, a separate entity — a butcher knife raised high.

With the young woman clinging to him, Morgan almost fell backward, but somehow his gun came up, pointing past her, and he shouted, *"Stop!"*

But the killer kept coming, the bobbing light some distance behind.

His cameraman!

The blade arced even higher up and, as it reached its apex, Morgan fired, a body shot because in this darkness the black stocking mask made a head shot tough. The killer took another step and Morgan, thinking he'd missed, tried again, another body shot — and this second try created a blossom of red, a scarlet boutonniere that graced his chest and immediately wilted.

The butcher knife tumbled from the attacker's fingers as he pitched forward, dead weight dropping to the ground.

The cameraman yelled, *"Beck!"*

The shouted name had a hollow sound in the night.

David Yarno dropped the small DV camera, which hit the ground, its light staying on and shining its impassive attention on the downed killer's face.

The other agents and the detectives had caught up by now, Prentiss and Warren immediately going to Bonder to pry the hysterical young woman off Morgan. The back of the black dress was sheared several places and she was bleeding.

As Reid, Gideon, Hotchner and Learman, weapons at the ready, surrounded the sprawl of the masked killer, their flashlight beams on him, the cameraman was already kneeling next to his fallen comrade.

David Yarno turned Becker Chapin over in his arms and removed the stocking mask. Chapin stared blankly at the moon, and the moon stared blankly back.

Morgan, on his feet now, was coming over; Yarno looked between Gideon and Reid to see the approaching Morgan, and the cameraman screamed, "You *monster!* You killed him! You fucking *monster!*"

Clicking the safety on, Morgan holstered his pistol.

"These night shoots *are* rough," Morgan told the surviving killer.

Yarno sobbed as he held his dead partner in his arms. "I loved you," he moaned. "I wish I'd told you, Beck, I should have told you . . . but I love you, man. . . ."

Gideon and Morgan exchanged glances. Neither could know that in the soundtrack of their minds, both men had suddenly heard Mickey and Sylvia singing "Love Is Strange."

CHAPTER ELEVEN

Like the other victims, Kathy Bonder had been in costume — a nun's habit, the wimple having blown off in the process of running from the attacker. Though she had been slashed twice, Kathy was otherwise all right physically, and the wounds — made through the costume — were minor, barely breaking the skin. Emotionally, of course, she would be dealing with this ordeal for years to come, perhaps for the rest of her life.

Such long-term ill effects aside, the young woman's parents were ecstatic to hear their daughter was alive and well, and rushed to the hospital to meet her.

Supervisory Special Agent Jason Gideon spoke to the Kansas City FBI contingent, Parker and Minet, and thanked them for their help. They and their associates were already tearing down their equipment and getting ready to call it a very long day.

Jareau accompanied the Bonders to the hospital, to help them start to deal with what their daughter would be going through in the days and nights ahead.

The crime scene team had found a ridiculous wealth of evidence scattered and splattered about the run-down mobile home. Among the most substantial, and easiest to catalogue, were both killers' laptop computers, a script for their "movie," and various knives and handcuffs — their nasty props. The footage they'd shot had not turned up yet; their "studio" remained to be found.

Morgan, Reid and Prentiss were packing up their equipment and materials. With one killer in custody, and the other in the morgue, they wouldn't be staying around Lawrence a lot longer.

Hotchner and Gideon sat in a dark booth watching Learman and Warren interview David Yarno, who had moved past his grief and into full self-protection mode; Yarno, his dark blond hair long and greasy, was seated at a table with Warren next to him, while Learman prowled the periphery.

Currently Yarno was talking a blue streak about how Chapin had been behind everything. After all, Chapin had been the director, hadn't he? And Chapin had forced David to film everything. Just like Chapin had forced David to help kidnap those homeless people. All at the threat of death.

As the interview continued, Gideon stuck his head out of the booth and called Reid over to join them.

"I need to know what's in this," Gideon said, handing Reid the confiscated screenplay. "And I need to know now."

Reid nodded, and began to peruse the document, *Final Cut* (with no writer credit), which at his 20,000 words a minute rate took the young profiler four and a half minutes. His report on the contents took about half that.

After the summary, Gideon said to Reid, "According to his parents, Becker Chapin was not exactly a straight A student. Cs at best. Hotch, what did Yarno's mother say about David?"

"Good grades," Hotchner said. "Very smart."

Gideon turned back to Reid. "What about the screenplay you just read?"

Reid shrugged. "Not likely to have been written by a C- student."

"Are you saying it's a good screenplay?"

Reid grinned; he looked about fifteen. "Oh, no — it's horrible! Misogynist, misanthropic trash. But what they filmed, they put on paper first; the crime scene unit will probably find storyboards."

"I wouldn't be surprised," Gideon said.

Reid's expression shifted, eyes narrowing, and now he looked his full twenty-five years. "What distinguishes the screenplay is not the quality of the writing. It's something else entirely."

"Go on."

"The grammar is all correct, the spelling too, the presentation well-organized. Even some of the ideas seem too . . . mature for an individual who was 'average,' if indeed Becker Chapin was even that."

Gideon flipped a hand. "Wasn't Quentin Tarantino a C student?"

"I don't know," Reid admitted. "Maybe you should check in with Garcia for that one."

"Thanks," Gideon told Reid with a smile.

"My pleasure. Sort of."

And Reid returned to packing up.

Gideon stood at the silvered window through which David Yarno could be seen chattering, blaming his late collaborator for everything short of the Kennedy assassination and global warming.

Gideon said to Hotchner, "Here we are, watching this kid talk about how innocent he is, how it was all Chapin's idea . . . making his friend, the average student, out as our mastermind. Which would make the smart kid, in this instance, the submissive one. How many times have you seen that?"

Hotchner's eyebrows rose and fell in a facial shrug. "Well, Leopold and Loeb were both smart. Leopold was in law school at nineteen and, at the time, Loeb was the youngest graduate in the history of the University of Michigan."

Gideon nodded, then he said, "Gerald and Charlene Gallego were a lot like this pair. Charlene claimed she was a battered wife, and only did what Gerald told her to stay alive. They kidnapped, raped and killed ten people, mostly teenage girls. He claimed she was a willing participant. Then, years later, she basically confessed to having been an equal partner."

Hotchner's eyes met Gideon's. "You think that's what we have here?"

"Maybe." Gideon nodded toward the glass. "I'd like to talk to David."

Ten minutes later, Learman and Warren took a break. When they came out, Gideon asked if he could have a pass at the suspect.

"Be our guest," Warren said.

"He's lying," Learman said bitterly. "He's as guilty as the dead one. But the little prick is good."

Gideon half smiled. "I'm better."

"Have at him," Learman said with a good-riddance wave.

Seated at the scarred brown interview-room table, David Yarno looked about as impressive as a kid working a take-out window.

Gideon sat down next to the young man, his back to the two-way window. He rested the copy of the screenplay on the table between them; it had been rolled up in Gideon's fist and now he smoothed it out.

"I've been watching," Gideon said easily, jerking a thumb toward the mirrorlike surface behind him.

David Yarno's brown eyes were big and bright and Gideon was reminded of the old Walter Keane paintings of big-eyed innocent children; but any look of innocence was undercut by the young man's mouth, which was a thin, cruel line.

"If you've been watching," Yarno said, "then you know I'm a victim in this, like that girl. Beck forced me, all the way. Man, I was scared of him. *Way* scared."

"I heard." Gideon tapped the screenplay. "It's all in here, too. Everything Beck thought, all his fantasies, his visions. It would have been quite a film if you two had finished it."

Yarno nodded. "It would've rocked. Takes

horror to a whole new level."

"You mean, by staging real kills?"

"Well, that wasn't my idea. He made me participate. But, yeah, it would've been real hardcore horror, our movie . . . 'cause it *was* real."

Gideon's manner was vaguely conspiratorial. "D'you wonder how we knew you two guys had kidnapped Kathy Bonder?"

The big brown eyes didn't blink much; but they blinked now. "How *did* you?"

Gideon shrugged. "Saw the poster in Beck's bedroom. Kathy Bonder is a dead ringer for the actress in *Il Morte Improvviso.*"

"That was Beck's idea. He wanted a cool-looking chick to star, and there was a resemblance. And Kathy's cool. He knew her from college, a little. Hey, I'm glad she's all right."

Gideon shifted in his chair. "And I think I know why you asked for that odd amount — $68,000."

"You do?"

The profiler nodded. "You ran overbudget, didn't you? You had a shortfall to make up."

Yarno grinned. "You're pretty smart, mister. Yeah, we ran overbudget, all right. Plus, there were some script changes. That was what we needed to finish the movie and, you know, take it around on the festival circuit."

Gideon raised his eyebrows. "You wanted to take *Final Cut* out to film festivals?"

"Sure! After Beck's film project, in college, got trashed by that professor? Beck, he figured he'd show that no-talent prof which of them *really* knew their shit about film."

"Sounds like Becker was a pretty angry guy."

"Yeah. Yeah, he was."

"What about you, David — are you angry?"

"Not really. I'm cool."

"Not even at Becker? For making you do all these terrible things you didn't want to do?"

The big brown eyes blinked again. "We were friends. Like brothers. You cut a brother a lot of slack, you know."

Gideon raised his eyebrows, spoke admiringly: "You know, a movie like this, taking it to the next level . . . and with the media attention that'll be attracted . . . Now that this is over, there's gonna be a lot written about it."

Yarno's eyes tightened. "Probably."

"In a way it's sad, Becker missing out."

"Missing out?"

Gideon nodded. "Oh yeah. On all the

fame. The glory. After all, *he* wrote and directed the film — *he's* the auteur of the piece. Lucky for you, you just filmed the murders. You said it yourself — really, you're just another victim." Gideon gave the boy a dreamy smile. "But in a weird way, it is kind of cool."

"What is?"

"Becker Chapin, this gifted filmmaker, this visionary, who died young? He'll be all over the news programs, they'll write books about him, make documentaries, maybe even make movies. Imagine that, a movie about Becker's movie! That'd really be something."

Yarno said nothing; he just stared at the screenplay.

Gideon tapped its cover again. "You know, Beck wrote a hell of a horror show. But in the end, David, you're better off a victim. Better a live nobody, than a dead superstar."

Yarno's fingers curled into fists.

"I wonder who they'll get to play Beck in the movie?" Gideon mused. Then he darkened his tone: "I wonder if your character will even be in it? Seems unfair."

Yarno's fists slammed down on the table. "That motherfucker didn't know which end of the camera to *point!* And if you think *he* wrote that, you're an idiot, too! His spelling sucked ass so bad, fuckin' *spell check* couldn't fix it!"

"What are you saying, David?"

Yarno grabbed the screenplay, hugged it to his bosom. "*I* wrote *Final Cut*! *I* directed it. Beck was just an actor — cattle, like Hitchcock said! I let the fucker act in *my* movie! He was Freddie Krueger, but *I* was Wes Craven!"

"Really? It's kind of hard to believe."

He sat forward, breathing hard. "Look, Beck knew movies, sure; him and me knew more about movies than anybody in that stupid film school, including the professor, that's for sure. Okay, so Beck had the idea to base our movie around our favorite scenes in cult flicks, right? But it was *my* idea to do real murder scenes, and give us both the chance to bring some of our favorite sick shit to life! Beck had no idea how to do it. I did. *I* did!"

"But wasn't Beck the strong one?" Gideon asked, in mock befuddlement. "Your protector?"

"Yeah — in junior fucking *high,* man! Since then, it's been my *brain,* not his fists, my *talent,* not his nerve, that got us where we are. Look, I loved the guy . . . but he wouldn't have been jack shit without me. Oh, he tried to do things on his own, like

315

that project he screwed up at college? His professor was right about that. I wrote *that* script, too, but 'cause it was for class, Beck said *he* had to direct it, right? Big talk. But like always, he fell down in the execution."

"The execution's no problem for you?"

"No. I'm a natural."

"Lucky for you." Gideon rose, his smile grim. "Because, David — execution is very likely where you're headed."

"Murder is unique
in that it abolishes the party it injures,"
the poet W.H. Auden said,
"so that society has to take the place
of the victim
and on his behalf demand atonement
or grant forgiveness;
it is the one crime
in which society has a direct interest."

EPILOGUE

The plane glided eastward, the morning sun lighting their way and glinting off the craft's sleek surface as they jetted home.

They were not in Kansas anymore. Good-byes had been said, and several on the team had noticed that Gideon and Detective Lucy Warren had stood chatting and exchanging contact info, in the most lingering of the farewells.

And skeptical Detective Rob Learman made a point of shaking every profiler's hand, and telling Hotch that "the BAU bunch" had made a believer out of him.

Everyone was properly exhausted. Jareau was sacked out on one of the couches, a thin blanket covering her. Prentiss curled up across the aisle reading a paperback: Kurt Vonnegut's *Mother Night*.

Ever the glutton for punishment, Hotchner sat in the next row back, tray table down, filling out reports. Morgan lounged across the aisle from him, his eyes closed but his head moving to the beat on his headset — classic Al Green.

In back, Gideon and Reid sat opposite, the latter listening to Miles Davis again, the former reading his favorite magazine, *British Birds* (not pornography: ornithology). Reid paused the mp3 player, slipped out his earbuds and sent his eyes Gideon's way until his mentor stopped reading and looked back.

"What?" Gideon asked.

"I don't understand our two killers," Reid said.

Gideon half-smiled. "Really? Your insights into their screenplay exposed David Yarno."

"I know. But Yarno, especially . . . he wasn't stupid. How could these two actually think people would perceive a snuff film as entertainment?"

"To some extent, people believe what they want to believe, in spite of the facts. When that reaches a delusional stage . . ."

"That's where we come in, I suppose."

"Sometimes," Gideon said. "Sometimes not. Delusional behavior doesn't necessarily lead to criminal acts."

"It did with our two frustrated filmmakers."

"Yarno and Chapin didn't have the talent

to bring a work of imagination to life; so they decided to invest their film with real life."

"Real *death.*" Reid shook his head. "To me, these killing teams are the hardest to comprehend."

"People come together because of mutual needs," Gideon said.

"Love, you mean."

"Yes. You often hear couples saying that their partner completes them. And that's often a wonderful thing. That's where family begins."

"Unless two twisted sets of needs give birth to murder."

Gideon shrugged. "Who knows? Maybe individually, these two boys would never have acted on their impulses to kill."

"Harmless chemicals," Reid said, "coming together to form nitroglycerine."

Gideon shifted in his seat. "Reid, every time we encounter one of these killing pairs, we learn about what makes them tick. Let's hope, the more we learn, the sooner we can start to hear the ticking before it turns into a full-fledged bomb."

Reid lifted his eyebrows, smiled nervously and his mentor smiled back and returned to his birds.

Slipping his earphones back in, Reid

settled back with Miles Davis again. He hit play — *In a Silent Way,* the song "Shhh/ Peaceful." The mood it conveyed helped.

But he still did not understand.

PROFILE IN THANKS

My assistant, Matthew Clemens, helped me develop the plot of *Jump Cut,* and worked up a lengthy story treatment (which included all of his considerable forensics research) from which I could work.

Profiler Steven R. Conlon, Assistant Director, Division of Criminal Investigation for the State of Iowa Department of Public Safety, generously provided a great deal of help and useful information.

Lt. Chris Kauffman (retired), Bettendorf (Iowa) Police Department and Lt. Paul Van Steenhuyse (retired), Scott County Sheriff's Office, provided professional insights and expertise.

The following books were consulted: *Profile of a Criminal Mind* (2003), Brian Innes; *Mindhunter* (1995), John Douglas and Mark Olshaker; and *My Life Among the Serial Killers* (2004), Helen Morrison with Harold Goldberg. Information was also gleaned

323

from Court TV's Crime Library.com, concerning killing teams, including Leopold and Loeb.

Special thanks go to Executive Producer Edward Allen Bernero of *Criminal Minds;* editor Kristen Weber of Penguin Putnam Publishing; and Maryann C. Martin of CBS Consumer Products. Without them, this novel series would not have happened.

Thanks also go to agent Dominick Abel; Matthew's wife, Pam Clemens, a knowledgeable *Criminal Minds* fan who really aided the effort; and the author's wife, Barbara Collins, whose eagle eye for typos, awkward phrases and inconsistencies is anything but criminal.

ABOUT THE AUTHOR

Max Allan Collins was hailed in 2004 by *Publishers Weekly* as "a new breed of writer." A frequent Mystery Writers of America "Edgar" nominee, he has earned an unprecedented fourteen Private Eye Writers of America "Shamus" nominations for his historical thrillers, winning for his Nathan Heller novels, *True Detective* (1983) and *Stolen Away* (1991).

His graphic novel *Road to Perdition* is the basis of the Academy Award–winning film starring Tom Hanks, directed by Sam Mendes. His many comics credits include the syndicated strip "Dick Tracy"; his own "Ms. Tree"; "Batman"; and "CSI: Crime Scene Investigation," based on the hit TV series for which he has also written video games, jigsaw puzzles, and a *USA Today* bestselling series of novels.

An independent filmmaker in the midwest, he wrote and directed the Lifetime movie *Mommy* (1996) and a 1997 sequel, *Mommy's Day.* He wrote *The Expert,* a 1995 HBO World Premiere, and wrote and directed the innovative made-for-DVD feature, *Real Time: Siege at Lucas Street Market* (2000). *Shades of Noir* (2004), an anthology of his short films, includes his award-winning documentary, *Mike Hammer's Mickey Spillane,* featured in a DVD collection of his films, *Black Box.* His most recent feature, *Eliot Ness: An Untouchable Life* (2006), based on his Edgar-nominated play, is also available on DVD.

His other credits include film criticism, short fiction, songwriting, trading-card sets, and movie/TV tie-in novels, including the *New York Times* bestseller *Saving Private Ryan.*

Collins lives in Muscatine, Iowa, with his wife, writer Barbara Collins. Their son Nathan, a recent University of Iowa graduate, has completed a year of post-grad studies in Japan.

The employees of Thorndike Press hope you have enjoyed this Large Print book. All our Thorndike and Wheeler Large Print titles are designed for easy reading, and all our books are made to last. Other Thorndike Press Large Print books are available at your library, through selected bookstores, or directly from us.

For information about titles, please call:
(800) 223-1244

or visit our Web site at:
www.gale.com/thorndike
www.gale.com/wheeler

To share your comments, please write:
Publisher
Thorndike Press
295 Kennedy Memorial Drive
Waterville, ME 04901

The Misinformation Age